Pretty Lips That Thugs Love

By: Twyla T

Copyright

Publishers Note

Published by Cole Hart Presents

This is a work of fiction. Names, characters, places, and events are strictly the product of the author or used fictitiously. Any similarities between actual persons, living or dead, events, settings, or locations are entirely coincidental.

Dedication

This book is dedicated to my big brother, Cornelius Jejuan Turner. I can literally write a whole book about this guy and how big his heart is, but I won't. I'll just keep it simple. If there is ever anything that I need, I know that he will make a way. We lost our dad at an early age, and although he can never take his place, that doesn't stop him from doing everything he can possibly can to take up the slack. Every time I have a book to come out, he buys it, reads the dedications and says, "I'm waiting on my shout out but I know you do stuff on your own time,"

You're right brother, and this one is for you! You told me to keep slanging them books because I do it so easy. It's not easy, but I'm definitely gonna keep moving forward. Thank you so much for all of your love and ongoing support. I love you!!

Acknowledgements

As always, I must acknowledge and thank God because without him, none of this would be possible. The ability to sit down and create enjoyable stories is so amazing. People often ask me, how do you come up with all of that stuff. The answer that comes out is, I don't even know. It just comes to me, but I had to catch myself recently and start saying, God because it's all him.

Shout out to Cole for keeping the covers and titles hot and always steering me in the right direction.

To every member of Twyla T's Reading Group and Cole Hart Signature Readers Club, Salute to you guys. Y'all are the real MVP's. I can always count on y'all to give it to me straight, no chaser and y'all know that's how I want it. It's very enjoyable to kick back, laugh, and have a good time with y'all. If you haven't checked out the Queens of Urban Fiction Anthology by Cole Hart Presents, go download that now so that you can see which hot stories are available and add them to your kindles.

As always, I put my all into it and I would love to have your honest feedback to help me excel in my passion. When you are done, please leave me a review on Amazon, Good Reads, and/or any of my social media pages so that I can read your feedback and make adjustments. My Facebook, Instagram, and Twitter handles are all @authortwylat

You may also email me at authortwylat@gmail.com

Search Twyla T's Reading Group on Facebook if you love my work and become a

supporter! We love to kick back and have fun in there, and there also random giveaways!

Other great reads by Author Twyla T:

We Both Can't Be Bae 1-3

I'll Never Love A Dope Boy Again 1 & 2

My Shawty 1-3 (An Original Love Story)

Chapter One

"Are you sure you wanna do this girl? I mean it's like murder ain't it?" Kya questioned her home girl Ashanti as she made the exit on Jack Warner Parkway in Tuscaloosa.

Ashanti really didn't want to have this conversation. She pondered over this pregnancy for a while now and she decided to do what was best for her.

Letting out a loud sigh, she said "Kya, you know Tay ain't bout to settle down and take care of no baby. Shit, I'll be stuck by my damn self and will be having to raise a kid alone. Besides, I'm almost four months pregnant so it's now or never and I pick now," Ashanti firmly stated.

Kya understood where her friend was coming from because she knew that Ashanti was speaking the truth about Tay.

"Aight… I feel you, but I hope Kentay's ass don't find out about this because I ain't got time for his bullshit, so we better hurry up," Kya replied while she was turning into the Women's Center. "Where's Raven at anyway? I thought she was bringing you," Kya continued while finding a place to park.

"She backed out since she's pregnant. Said she didn't feel right bringing me. I understand why," Ashanti replied as she nodded her head towards the parking lot. They looked at the protestors lined up marching and holding signs. Kya looked like she wanted to say something but kept her mouth closed. Looking at the protestors for another second, Ashanti turned her head away from the window and concentrated back on the task at hand. Ashanti didn't give a fuck about the protestors because she saw them the week before when she had her first appointment. Why she had to go through two appointments was still crazy to her, she inwardly thought. However, she reminded herself that she had to do what she had to do because Tuscaloosa was closer than Memphis.

Ashanti was having second thoughts about going through the with procedure and just keeping her baby because she didn't really want to go through an abortion, but she knew having a baby at the moment just wasn't in the plans. Ashanti knew that Kentay wouldn't do right no matter how many promises he made and even though she was going to school less than an hour away from home, she would make the best of her scholarship at Mississippi State University. Scoring a 25 on her ACT allowed her to pick pretty much any school she wanted, but Ashanti always wanted to attend State. It was sentimental to her since her dad graduated from there, and he died when she was ten.

Before they could get out of the car, Kya's little white Honda Civic started shaking as a reaction from the booming sound system of a truck that had pulled up right behind them. The way the truck was angled, it was clear that the owner was making sure they couldn't get away. The windows were tinted so black, even the back one which was facing Ashanti, that you couldn't see who was inside. She did notice that there were no tags on it yet, and she silently prayed Tay hadn't went and bought a new vehicle. Ashanti stared at the candy red Hummer sitting on 26's and a lump formed in her throat and her heart starting pounding hard in her chest when her boyfriend Kentay prepared to exit the vehicle. Both Ashanti and Kya were shocked and in total disbelief to see Tay walking towards their vehicle.

"Fuck! That prayer didn't get answered. How did he know where I was?" Ashanti spewed through gritted teeth to her girl who had just gotten out of the driver seat. Kya shrugged and ignored the question as she exited her car. She discreetly turned her camera on record mode because she knew some shit was about to pop off that would be worth capturing.

Kentay walked slowly towards Ashanti with *Trap Queen* by Fetty Wap blasting through the sound system. The expression on his face let her know that he was pissed the fuck off. Trying to buy herself some time and distance from him, Ashanti frantically began talking.

"What are you doing here? How did you find me? How did you know I was pregnant?" she asked, not giving him a chance to answer the first question. She noticed that he wasn't trying to answer her questions, so Ashanti tried to turn and walk the other way. However, she was too slow and didn't get away quick enough. Kentay didn't give one fuck about where he was and what he was about to do. Before Ashanti knew it, he snatched her up and threw her against the car and began choking her.

"I know good and got damn well you ain't bout to kill my mu'fuckin baby!" he spat as his grip became tighter and tighter around her neck. Ashanti couldn't answer even if she wanted to because his grip was so strong. The only thing she could do was claw at him and tried to pry his hands from cutting off her passage of air. The more she fought, the tighter his grip became so she finally succumbed to his wrath. After realizing that she had stopped struggling, Tay let her and Ashanti dropped to the ground in a coughing fit. Ashanti rubbed her neck while still coughing, trying her best to ease the pain. She knew there would be marks on her bronze color skin because she bruised easily.

Kentay stared down at her trying to calm himself and to get control of his emotions. Meanwhile, Kya recorded everything from the opposite side of the car while his homeboy, Slick, sat in the passenger seat of his truck smoking on some Kush and talking on the phone. Having witness these types of shenanigans between Kentay and Ashanti before, Slick shook his head at his friend and continued his conversation. For that reason alone, Slick knew exactly what was going on but dared not to intervene because it wasn't his business.

Moments later, Ashanti got her breathing back under control but remained sitting on the ground. When Ashanti looked up, she stared at the man that she loved with her whole heart as he towered down over her with his six-foot frame. As pissed off as she was, she couldn't help but to stare at everything that she fell in love with about him. His muscular frame turned her on from the jump, along with his dark brown bedroom eyes and smooth golden skin. Kentay was a ladies' man no doubt, but Ashanti couldn't resist his charm. He always wore a serious expression on his face, and people knew not to fuck with him. Shaking and trembling from the inside out, Ashanti was scared to death because it was the first time she had been on the receiving end of his wrath in that manner. She wasn't sure of what he would do next, so she decided to just stay still.

After what seemed like an eternity, Kentay bent down and pulled Ashanti up roughly.

"If you ever try to do some shit like this again, I'll kill yo ass. You know I love you, and I'ma always hold you down so stop tripping and shit. Now give me a kiss with them big, juicy ass lips," he said, speaking to her as if she was a child and pulled Ashanti's body closer to him and gripped her thick hips and fat ass. Ashanti didn't know how to respond, so she just remained quiet. Tay had her five foot five inch framed pulled close to him so he couldn't see the tears that were threatening to fall.

After a few moments, Tay finally noticed the fear in her eyes, and he tried to soothe her as best he could.

"I'm sorry baby, but you know how I get when you act crazy," Tay told her and kissed those luscious lips that he loved so much. Ashanti yielded to him without putting up much of a fuss. He rubbed his hands all over her body, giving her ass and hips extra attention like they were at home instead of outside in the parking lot of a Women's Clinic. For some reason, Shanti just couldn't shake Tay. It was probably because he was all that she knew.

"Yo Slick, hop in with Kya while my baby get in wit me," Kentay said to his homeboy. Slick nodded his head in understandment and made the move to switch vehicles. Tay ushered Ashanti to the passenger side and helped her to get in the truck. As Ashanti put her seatbelt on, Kya walked over to the truck, and Ashanti rolled the window down.

"Call me later boo," Kya said with much concern and gave Ashanti her iPhone and purse that she had dropped on the ground. Unable to speak, Ashanti gave Kya a nod, took her stuff and placed them in her lap.

Kentay pulled out of the parking lot and starting riding with both of them deep into their own thoughts. With her head resting on the seat and eyes closed, Ashanti prayed that having this baby would make Tay do right by her, but deep down she felt like it was only going to add to their problems.

"I can't believe you was bout to kill my seed ma. I expect that type of shit from these hoes out in the streets, but not you," Kentay said in a tone filled with shock and disgust, finally breaking the silence after riding for about fifteen minutes.

"Tay, it's not like our relationship is perfect," Ashanti replied after a few more moments of silence.

"Ain't no relationship perfect, but communication is everything. Don't ever do no shit like this again. I got you, and I got my lil man no matter what," he told her and reached over and rubbed her stomach.

"How you know it's a boy?" Ashanti asked while smiling.

"I just know," Kentay answered and smirked.

Silence filled the truck once more. It wasn't until then that Ashanti noticed that they weren't headed back towards home; instead, they were on Interstate 20 going east. Taking a peak in her direction, he could see confusion written all over her.

"Just sit tight. I got you," Tay said and kept driving. Before she knew it, Ashanti had dosed off. When she woke up, Tay was turning off of 459. Looking in Tay's direction, she smiled and started feeling excited because she'd figured out where they were heading. Ashanti knew he was going to the restaurant she mentioned to him the last time they rode through Birmingham. Ashanti loved Italian food and mentioned Gianmarco's Restaurant to Tay because of the great reviews. That was about six months ago, and she had forgotten about it. Evidently he hadn't.

They walked in and were seated within five minutes. It was fifteen minutes after eleven, so they beat the lunch hour crowd and placed their orders right away. When the waitress walked away,

Kentay pulled a box out of his pocket. Ashanti's hands went straight over her mouth.

"Oh my gawwddd!!" Ashanti squeaked when he opened the box and laid eyes on the platinum diamond ring.

"Wait a minute... calm down baby!" Kentay said trying to keep her from jumping the gun. "This ain't no engagement ring. It's a friendship ring. I'm only twenty-three and you eighteen so ain't neither one of us ready for marriage, but as long as you wearing this ring, I got you," he told her. Tears were forming in Ashanti's eyes.

"It's beautiful baby," she finally said. "I just want you to stay committed to me," Ashanti continued.

"I got you baby. I'm working on getting better for you," Kentay replied.

"I hope so baby, but don't do it for me. Do it for you. I can't keep going back and forth with all of these thots tryna prove my love when I shouldn't have to," Ashanti retorted.

"I know. You've been holding me down for almost three years, and I appreciate you. This is my way of moving in the right direction. It ain't gon happen overnight, but we gon get there. I love you girl," Tay sincerely replied. He knew that Ashanti had to do a lot of sneaking and going against what her mother said to be with him, so he told himself that it was time to step up and do right by her. Ashanti finally noticed two keys hanging from the ring after picking it up and out of the box, and was shocked.

"What are the keys for?" she inquired.

"When we leave here, I'ma show you," he told her.

After finishing their delicious meals, Kentay paid the bill and they left. Ashanti wasted no time posting her ring on every social media site she had an account for as soon as she got settled in the truck. Her notifications were blowing up on Facebook, Snap Chat, Instagram, and Twitter. She captioned the picture with the hashtags #HisForever #ImWifey #PleaseBelieveIt and also took an off guard picture of him driving and tagged him on Facebook. Kentay barely got on Facebook, but Ashanti tagged him in pictures so the hoes would know she wasn't going anywhere. The crazy thing about their relationship is that she never caught him cheating. However, there was always a different female calling and texting Ashanti about Tay, so she knew for them to be that bold, something had to be going on no matter how much he denied it.

Two hours later, Kentay lightly shook Ashanti after he parked. Ashanti didn't even realize she had gone to sleep. When she focused, she wondered what in the world they were

doing at Carpenter Place. They were parked at the new condos on Louisville Street in Starkville.

"What are we doing here?" Shanti inquired.

"Get out and let's see. Be sure you grab those keys," he told her. Ashanti got out behind Kentay and followed him. They were parked in front of building G, which was in the back, and Kentay stopped at door number four. Ashanti put one of the keys in the lock and it opened. When she walked inside, her mouth hit the floor. The place looked like it came straight off of HGTV. The wooden floors were glistening and the living area was very spacious. Ashanti could see the beautiful marble top on the island and fell in love with it instantly. An 80-inch flat screen was mounted on the wall with a sound bar connected to it. Ashanti walked slowly through the place not believing it could get any better, but she was wrong. She walked into the master bedroom and slipped off her shoes because the carpet was so pretty and white. It felt like cotton in between her toes. There was a California King bed in the center of the floor, and it was already decorated in red and black. The bathroom had a walk in shower, a Jacuzzi, his and her sinks and it was color coordinated with the décor from the bedroom.

Realizing she hadn't said a word since she entered the apartment, she turned towards Kentay.

"Baby is this our place?" Ashanti finally asked after doing a complete walk through of the entire condo.

"It's yours. Everything here is in your name. Of course I'll be here, but it's all yours baby. I know you going to school here, so you need to be close to campus instead of driving back and forth," he smiled and told her.

Not sure of what to say, Ashanti said the first thing that came to her mind.

"Well you know my motor went out in my car so I was gonna stay on campus anyway," she responded with total surprise still lacing her voice.

"I got that taken care of too," Kentay said proudly and pulled a key out of his pocket and handed it to her.

"You bought me a car too?" Ashanti excitedly questioned. "Where is it?" she asked and started walking towards the front.

"Hit the alarm," Tay replied. Ashanti quickly opened the door and looked out to see which vehicle the key belonged to.

BEEP! BEEP!

She did as he said and the alarm beeped to a brand new red 2016 Range Rover.

"Oh my gawwddd!! You bought me a Range," Ashanti screamed and ran and hopped in. Her name was engraved in the steering wheel as well as the custom made floor mats. She checked out all of the features while Kentay stood there smiling at her. "Baby, I can't believe you did all of this for me. Thank you so much," Ashanti cried and tears started streaming down her face.

"You're welcome baby girl. It's the least I can do. I give different kids scholarships for college all the time, so what I look like not making sure my girl and my baby are taken care of?" Tay replied. Ashanti got out of the truck and kissed him sensually.

After kissing for what seemed like forever, Kentay pulled his lips from Ashanti, trying to get some much needed air.

"Damn, you got my dick hard as fuck. You bout to throw me off track. I gotta go and take care of some business, but you keep my pussy wet for me. I'll be back later," Tay told her and kissed her again and squeezed her ass before hopping in his Hummer and leaving. Ashanti was smiling from ear to ear when she went back in and walked around her new place. "I knew he loved me. Things are starting to look up thanks to you," she cooed to the baby while rubbing her stomach.

Chapter Two

After putting a smile on Ashanti's face, Tay headed out to Black Jack to take care of some business. Kentay was the man in the Golden Triangle area. As much as he tried not to be flashy, he just couldn't help himself. He was proud of the name he built for himself over the years. Ten years ago, at the tender age of thirteen, Tay started running the streets. He caught his first body six short months after that. Nino, the old head he was running for, took care of everything and instilled in him ways to never get caught. Since the relationship Tay had with his dad was pretty much nonexistent, he looked up to Nino, and in return, Nino treated him like the son he never had. When Nino died five years ago, his entire empire fell into the hands of eighteen year old Kentay Mills. Since he had been properly groomed, the transition was sweet. Many hated on him, but he didn't have one fuck to give. All he wanted to do was make money and help people, whether it was putting them on to work or through scholarships and other services he provided throughout the community and state.

Many looked at Kentay as a hypocrite because the same shit that he was selling was what took his mom out years ago. He remembered May 10, 2005 like it was yesterday.

It was a hot and humid day when Kentay and Slick left school Thursday afternoon, but it didn't keep them from going to their favorite spot on the West Side to shoot basketball. They walked from school up on Henderson Hill and went straight to the court. Both of them loved the game and had plans on trying out for the middle school basketball team at Armstrong the next year. Slick had his basketball, dribbling between his legs and Tay went in for the steal and succeeded. He took the ball and ran to the court and dunked it.

"You better tighten up or I'ma rip you every time man," Tay said to his boy semi-bragging, but also schooling him. They ended up playing one on one until the crowd showed up, and then the full court games began.

Kentay and Slick always played on the same team and everyone knew it, but that never stopped the hating. They had become immune to it and didn't entertain it because Slick's mom was strict on him and would make him come straight home if he got into any kind of trouble. Kentay on the other hand, his mom never forced him to be home at a certain time. Out of respect for his friend, he still tried to keep his anger in check and ignore the assholes to stay out of trouble because they always had each other's back.

The day went well on the court, like it pretty much always did. About six o'clock, Kentay started walking with Slick towards his house. Kentay lived in Brooksville Garden, which was known as The Garden around town. However, they bypassed it and headed towards Reed's Place, which was on down the road so that Slick could get home on time. Slick obeyed the rules as much as possible and tried not to argue with his mom because he didn't like to put extra stress on her. Although she never said it, she stressed every single day over his dad. Slick's nickname was given to him after his dad, who was serving a twenty-five year bid in prison for a string of crimes that consisted of carjacking, bank robberies, and breaking and entering. Not many knew what his real name was because he hated it, but even the ones who did called him Slick after his dad because he looked exactly like him. Suzanne, Slick's mom, hated that nickname, but there was nothing she could do to stop the name. She vowed to make sure her son stayed on the straight and narrow, which was why she was so strict.

When they made it to her house, she invited Kentay in for dinner, just like she always did. He sat down and ate chicken and rice with them before heading home.

"I'll see you tomorrow man," Kentay said to Slick after he finished eating and got up to leave. "Thanks for dinner Mrs. Hudson," he told Suzanne and gave her a hug before leaving. During the walk home, Tay made a pit stop by the store to grab some red Kool-Aid. He knew his mom probably wasn't home yet, so he wasn't in a hurry. It was almost nine o'clock by the time he made it home. Using his key, he went inside and an eerie feeling came over him. Brushing it off, he went straight to the kitchen to make the

Kool-Aid. As soon as he started ripping the Kool-Aid packages open, Tay heard a loud noise coming from the back.

What the hell he thought to himself and went and grabbed the bat that was placed behind the front door before going to check things out. Walking quietly towards the back, Kentay gripped the bat tight, ready to bust someone's skull. He heard some faint moans coming from towards the bathroom and rushed in with the bat midair. When he saw who it was, he dropped the bat immediately and ran to his mother's side. Looking beside her on the floor, he knew exactly what was going on, but said a prayer that his mom would be okay. He turned the water on in the tub, took the shower head and started spraying cold water on her face. When she didn't move after several moments, he ran and called 911.

Less than fifteen minutes later, everyone was outside being nosey as paramedics rolled Kenya out of the house on the gurney covered with a white sheet. Mrs. Suzanne took Kentay in, but he just didn't want to live there forever. He turned to the streets a year later and never looked back. Slick was true to his boy and rode with him, disobeying his mother for the first time. The bond they shared was unbreakable.

The ringing of Kentay's phone broke him from his thoughts.

"What up?" he answered.

"You coming through?" the voice on the other end asked. He hesitated for a moment, but finally answered.

"Yeah, I'm on my way. We need to talk," he replied and hung up without waiting for a reply. He turned his music up and blasted *YFN* by Lucci while on his way to The Links.

It's either now or never

Right now I'm high as ever

One of the hottest ever

I'm just being modest

I'mma be the topic

They talk about forever

When they ask about me

Just make sure you tell em

We just some young fly niggas (Yeah)

We just some young fly niggas (Yeah)

We just some young fly niggas (Yeah)

Kentay pulled up to his destination thirty minutes later. For some strange reason, he was nervous, but he knew that he needed to get inside and handle his business. Before he could even knock, the door swung open, and he was greeted by a smiling face. She knew exactly what he liked, so she wasted no time unbuckling his pants and pushing him towards the sofa.

"Wait… wait," he started to say.

"Let me take care of you and then we can talk," she replied.

"What the hell," he told himself and laid back and got ready to enjoy the bomb ass head that he was about to receive. Kentay's dick was already standing at attention before he felt her tongue teasing his tip. Being a sucker for a woman with a fat ass who could give some fye head was one of his weaknesses, and the girl who sucking his dick like she taught Super head her skills knew just that.

"Ohhh shiiittt!" Kentay moaned while receiving some superb dome.

"You like that baby?" she asked him, knowing good and damn well he was enjoying every second of it. A few minutes later, Kentay felt his nut rising and tried to get up, but he was held in place and all of his future kids went straight down her throat. She swallowed them with a smile plastered on her face.

"Got damn girl!" he huffed and laid his head back. He knew she was ready to fuck, but he just couldn't do it. Sleeping with her had been a mistake that turned into mistake after mistake at least three times a week for the past few months. He blamed the very first time on his drunkenness. After that though, there was no excuse and he knew it, which was why he was about to end things once and for all.

After going to the bathroom to gather himself, Kentay walked back out ready to deliver the speech that he had rehearsed in his head over and over and over.

"Why you hop up so fast? You know if I coulda hopped on it, I would have," she told him.

"Listen, we gotta stop this. It's not cool, and I gotta take a stand. I didn't intend to come here and get my dick sucked, but it is what it is. I don't want anyone to get hurt, and if we keep this up that's exactly what is gonna happen so we gotta end this shit. It's foul on all levels, and I can't keep doing this to my girl. We bout to be a real family. I hope you understand, and I truly hope you feel the same way," Kentay said as nicely as he could.

"Your girl? You weren't thinking about your girl while ramming your dick in me these last few months. But for real though, why you wanna end something this good? Besides, I love you," she confessed.

"Ain't no way you love me. That's just lust because I been dicking you down with this anaconda, but we can't do it no mo. Real talk," he told her. When he noticed the tears welling up in her eyes, he tried to continue being nice, but knew he had to be firm. "Hey, you need to focus on your family. You got a baby on the way and a nice standup guy. Be the woman he needs you to be," Kentay pleaded and turned towards the door to leave. Not giving in so easily, she confessed something that she had been keeping close to her chest.

"But my baby is yours Tay," she sobbed and his hand froze on the doorknob.

Chapter Three

Ashanti couldn't contain her excitement after Tay left, so she decided she would fix a nice candlelight dinner to show her appreciation. When she went into the kitchen and looked in the cabinets and refrigerator, everything was fully stocked, and it made her smile that much more. Her massive walk-in closet in the master bedroom was already full of clothes, but she still needed to go to her mom's house in Weir and gather some of her favorite items. After pulling out a few items she needed to prepare dinner, Ashanti grabbed her cell phone and called her mom. She already knew how the conversation was going to go, but decided it was time to get it over with.

"Hey Shanti… are you on your way home? I need you to grab some Clorox for me," her mom Tina asked as soon as she answered after two rings.

"Hey mom! I wasn't planning on coming today, but if you need it today I can get Kya to drop it by there," Ashanti replied.

"You just don't spend no time at home. You already bout to go to college in a couple of months. I thought you would be home more after graduation, but let me guess, you with that thug," Tina stated.

"He's not a thug mom, but I was calling to give you some good news," Ashanti stated defending her baby's daddy.

"Hmph… I just call it like I see it. You been running behind that boy these past few years just going damn crazy," Mrs. McNeal said.

"Anyways mom… I got a new condo… and you're also about to be a grandma," Ashanti nervously said in a rushed tone. A silent pause met Ashanti on the other end of the line. Tina was so quiet that Ashanti had to pull her cell phone away from her ear to make sure that her mom hadn't hung up on her. "Did you hear me mom?" Ashanti asked after the line was silent for a few moments.

"I heard you. I'm just a bit shocked at the last statement. You know how hard it was for me having you at a young age. I just thought that you would make better choices than me. Did the thug try to make you have an abortion?" Tina revolted.

"No mom, he didn't. We are doing good right now. He got me my own place, and the lease is in my name. I wish you would come to Starkville and visit," Ashanti said, feeling hopeful.

"Well, I'll definitely be by there, but I wish you were staying in a dorm and getting the full college experience. But with a baby on the way, I guess you need your own space. How far along are you anyway?" her mom asked.

"Four months," Ashanti mumbled, but her mom heard her loud and clear.

"FOUR MONTHS?! Really Ashanti? FOUR MONTHS?" Mrs. McNeal screamed.

"I know mom… I didn't want to tell you like this, but I didn't want you to find out from anyone else. I'm about to cook so I'll call you later," Ashanti said and rushed off of the phone to prevent hearing further disappointment in her mom's voice.

While the steaks were cooking, Ashanti whipped up some loaded mashed potatoes and asparagus. Since they had eaten Italian food earlier, she decided this would be the perfect meal to break in her new place. Figuring she could pass a little time, Ashanti grabbed her phone and logged onto Snap Chat and started viewing stories. When she noticed clips of the incident from earlier with Tay, she became pissed off and called Kya right away.

"Bitch, why the fuck you post that shit on Snap Chat?" Shanti spat as soon as her girl answered the phone.

"Bitch, we always play bout shit like that. Why you mad now?" Kya asked, surprised that Ashanti sounded angry and would call her about the video.

"That nigga choked me up so what was even funny about that? Yeah we post crazy shit all the time but I didn't record or post shit when Ryan went upside your head," Ashanti fumed.

"I'll delete the shit. I wasn't being funny damn," Kya compromised.

"All your damn followers prolly done saw the shit bout now and shared it. Snap Chat messy asses let you share other people's stories without you even knowing now remember," Ashanti said while shaking her head.

"Damn, I forgot all about that. I wasn't thinking and it was just a joke. I figured you woulda saw it by now anyway. What you been doin?" Kya inquired trying to take the heat off of her ass.

Ashanti filled Kya in on everything that happened after they parted ways and told her that her that she was shocked she didn't see the pictures all over social media. Kya informed her that she logged off right after posting on Snap Chat and went to visit a friend. They talked a little more about meeting up the next day to finalize everything for Raven's baby shower that would occur in just a few days, and then they hung up. Ashanti heard the door slam just as she was taking the garlic bread out of the oven and smiled.

"Damn, it smells good in here," Kentay said walking into the kitchen.

"You're right on time baby," Ashanti bragged and kissed him when he pulled her in for a hug.

"I'ma go hop in the shower right quick. I'll be back," Tay told her. Before she could reply, her phone rang and she answered.

"Hello, what's up chic? You gon live a long time, I was just talking bout you girl," Ashanti greeted.

"Oh yeah? You and who? Your punk ass boyfriend?" Raven asked in an annoyed voice.

"Watch your mouth talking about my boo… but nah I was talking to Kya," Ashanti defensively replied. "You ready for Saturday?" she continued ignoring her friend's mood.

"Yes! I'm so excited. I still don't know why y'all wouldn't let me help with the planning," Raven whined.

"We got you girl… besides, you'll get to plan mine next," Ashanti excitedly stated.

"Oh my gawdd… What? You pregnant" Raven said as sarcastically as she could.

"Damn! You got jokes like you didn't know. What the hell is wrong wit you?" Ashanti asked slightly offended.

"Nothing girl, I was just joking don't act so uptight," Raven muffled while trying to reign in her emotions.

"Well… let me get done with dinner before Tay gets outta the shower," Ashanti responded still confused by her friend's reaction.

"That nigga probably been fucking someone else if he came in and got straight in the shower. You better check him," Raven confidently stated.

"Bye Raven," Ashanti snapped, becoming frustrated and hung up.

When Kentay walked back into the dining area, he immediately noticed that Ashanti's mood had slightly changed by the expression on her face.

"What's wrong babe?" he asked her.

"Nothing, let me fix our plates." Ashanti tried to ignore her emotions and got up from the table.

"Nah I got it. You cooked, so just relax and I'll fix em," Tay said and headed into the kitchen.

Ashanti sat back down and waited while Kentay fixed the plates. She pondered on whether or not she was going to address her feelings. Raven always said slick shit about Kentay and Ashanti didn't understand why.

"I know this bout to be good," Tay said as he sat Ashanti's plate in front of her and then sat his across from her and took his seat. "So what's wrong babe? We said we was gonna communicate better and shit. You was fine when I walked in and now you looking like you been sucking on lemons," Tay said after taking a couple of bites of food.

"Raven," Ashanti said barely audible and Kentay dropped his fork.

"What about her?" he asked after regaining his composure.

"She's always throwing shade and shit. Here I am planning her baby shower, and she talking about if you came home and hopped right in the shower, you was probably just out fucking another bitch," Ashanti stated.

"She's jealous. I still don't know why you deal with her, but I can't choose your friends for you," Kentay said trying to play off his growing anger.

"We've been friends forever. I know she had her ways, but I do love her and want her in my life. She's been there for me through some of my hardest times just like I have been for her," Shanti replied.

"Well, we not bout to let her mess up our night. The day started out shaky and shit, but it turned out for the best, so let's finish this bomb ass meal you cooked and then we can relax," Tay retorted.

"You're right baby. That's why I love you," Ashanti happily declared.

"I love you too girl," he told her and then dived back into his meal.

When they finished eating, Kentay led Ashanti to the master bathroom and started running water so that she could soak in the Jacuzzi. He slowly undressed her and admired her body and rubbed her stomach that had a small pudge.

"All this time, I thought you were just getting thicker, but you're carrying my son," he said and bent down and kissed her stomach. He assisted her with getting stepping in the Jacuzzi and then sat on the side and started rubbing her shoulders. Thinking about the event from that morning, Ashanti wanted to know the answers to her question.

So as she relaxed, she said "Babe, how did you know where I was this morning anyway?" Ashanti asked with her eyes closed while enjoying his strong hands massaging her shoulders.

"We just gon leave that in past baby," he replied with the best answer that he could think of. He didn't want to reveal his source as it would undoubtedly lead to more questions.

Ashanti dropped the subject because she wanted to keep the atmosphere pleasant. After Kentay finished massaging her and washing her off, he scooped her up and wrapped a towel around her body.

"The parts that the towel didn't dry, I'ma lick it off," he whispered to her and placed her in the middle of the California King. Ashanti shivered with pleasure as she looked into Tay's eyes because she knew what was about to happen and she couldn't wait. After Kentay slipped his clothes off, he climbed in the bed in his birthday suit and kissed Ashanti's pretty lips sweetly while his hands roamed all over her tender body. He began making a trail of kisses down her body, not missing one spot. When he reached her breasts, he gave both of them the same amount of attention before moving further south.

When Kentay reached Shanti's wet mound, he inserted two fingers before nibbling on her clit, causing her juices to flow instantly. One of the things that she loved about Kentay was he always knew exactly what she needed. There were times when she wanted to be made love to like he was doing at the moment, and then there were times when she wanted to be fucked. She would get that the next morning. Getting lost in her thoughts, Ashanti felt Tay's rock hard dick easing into her tightness. She gasped as he entered. They had fucked and made love countless of times, but it still always took a few moments for her to get used to his ten inches penetrating her every single time.

After he stroked her slowly a few times, Ashanti started rotating her hips and matching Kentay thrust for thrust.

"Umm... shit! You feel so good baby," Ashanti moaned while pulling Tay closer to her.

"Not as good as you. You bet not ever give my pussy away! You hear me?" Tay demanded while deep stroking her.

"I... I... won't baby!" Ashanti stuttered.

"Whose pussy is this?" he asked while pounding her.

"It's yours... all yours daddy!" Shanti said while digging her nails into his back.

"It better be. Now flip that ass over and back it up on this dick," Tay told her and she happily obliged.

Ashanti knew that Tay loved hitting it from the back, but she also knew that he wouldn't last long with her throwing it back at him. She twerked on his dick and then creamed all over it before he shot what seemed like a pound of cum in her.

"Got damn... if you wasn't already pregnant you damn shol woulda got pregnant off of that," Tay chuckled and collapsed beside her on the bed. They both laughed as they cuddled. "You need to make an appointment and let me know when it is. We gotta make sure our son is Gucci," Tay said while rubbing her stomach.

"I'll call first thing in the morning," Shanti sleepily replied.

"Cool... now get some rest because I'm tired as fuck," Tay said, then closed his eyes. Ashanti smiled and was happy about the turn of events in her life. She silently thanked God and snuggled closer to Kentay and then drifted off to sleep.

Chapter Four

Ashanti had settled into her new place quite well. The day before, her mom came to visit and was impressed with the condo and with Kentay's taste in style. Tina made it known that she still didn't care for his ways and felt that her daughter could do better, but she vowed not to interfere in their relationship. Ashanti and her mom, along with Kya, finished picking up last minute items for Raven's baby shower the day before. It was a great day for the three, but now it was just Ashanti and her mom on campus at Mississippi State getting ready to register Ashanti for her fall classes. Kya was currently in Oxford doing the same thing because she received a full scholarship from Ole Miss. They knew the two schools hated each other, but told each other they wouldn't let that interfere with their friendship.

"I'm loving this ride. Never thought I would ride, let alone drive a Range Rover," Tina exclaimed while exiting off of Highway 82 and heading towards campus.

"I'll buy you one in the future," Ashanti said trying to suck up to her mom who had been fussing at her all day. The closer they got to Garner Hall, which was where the Financial Aid office was, the thicker the traffic became.

"I still hate I don't get to help you move into a dorm and everything," Tina said to her daughter while maneuvering her way around and finally pulling into a parking space.

Honk. Honk. Honk.

A lady in a white Toyota Camry was blowing her horn like crazy. Tina never noticed her waiting for the parking space she had eased into until she started blowing her horn. When the two women locked eyes, the lady flipped Tina off and called her a bitch.

"Oh I know that bitch didn't just call me a bitch!" Tina stated while putting the truck in park.

31

"Mom… please just let it go," Ashanti pleaded with her mom because she knew her mom would fight in a heartbeat if she felt disrespected. Luckily, the lady left the parking lot so they didn't see her when they got out.

Everything went well with getting Ashanti registered. They ran into a small road bump when it was stated that all freshmen had to live on campus. But at the moment, the waiting list for the freshmen dorms were full. Once Ashanti mentioned her pregnancy and her mom was adamant about her having her own space, everything was resolved. Ashanti knew the campus well already, but she decided to walk around with her mom and continue spending time with her.

"Ooooh girl there go Ahmad," Ashanti heard a girl nearby say while giggling. Ashanti had no idea who they were talking about, but when she looked ahead and saw a sexy ass chocolate man coming towards the direction she was walking in, her mouth instantly flew open. She couldn't help but to notice and admire his muscular body that was tatted up to perfection. He had on a tank top and was dribbling a basketball, so Ashanti figured that he must play basketball. The presence that the Ahmad guy had was indescribable to Ashanti. She had no idea that she was staring so hard and had stopped in front of them until her mom nudged her.

"I wish that damn Kentay could see you drooling over this young man here," Tina laughingly said causing Shanti to snap back to reality after nudging her didn't fully work.

"Shit… I mean shoot!" Ashanti said when she noticed Ahmad staring at her too.

"Hello Miss Beautiful… are you sisters new on campus?" Ahmad said to Tina and Ashanti causing them both to blush.

"See, this is the kinda man you need instead of that no good ass…" Tina started saying before Ashanti called her name and bumped her, cutting her off.

"Mom!" Ashanti screamed while trying to cover her face from the embarrassment her mom was causing.

"Well, I'm just telling the truth," her mom firmly stated. "Thank you for the compliment handsome young man," Tina said directing her attention to Ahmad.

He told Tina thanks, but for some reason he couldn't take his eyes off of Ashanti. They stared at each other for what seemed like an eternity, but in reality, it was only about ten seconds.

"I heard the girls back there call you Ahmad. We didn't formally meet, but it was good seeing you. We gotta get going now," Ashanti said and started walking away.

"Hold up! You're not going to tell me your name? Well… Hopefully I'll see you around campus," Ahmad said.

"I doubt it, I'm not staying on campus," Ashanti hurriedly stated refusing to give her name and continued trying to get away.

"Well be sure you come to my games. I think you gon be my good luck charm," Ahmad grinned to Ashanti. She heard him, but decided to ignore him because she felt guilty for the feelings she was having. She also heard him start talking to the girls who had been giggling about him and called them groupies in her head while rolling her eyes.

"Slow down Shanti… damn," her mom fussed after finally catching up with her.

"It's hot and I'm tired," Ashanti whined.

"No, you just don't know how to feel after being attracted to someone else besides that asshole," Tina fussed.

"Mooommm, please don't start. I don't even know that boy and I'm not attracted to him," Ashanti bellowed, trying to convince herself more than her mom because she knew that her mom always saw through most of her bullshit.

They left campus and headed to Harvey's to grab something to eat. On the way to the restaurant, Ashanti couldn't get Ahmad out of her head. Curiosity was getting the best of her, so she pulled her iPhone out of her purse and googled the basketball team. Sure enough, there he was. His profile read:

Ahmad Jones

Sophomore

Shooting Guard

6'3, 205 pounds

Hometown: Brandon, Mississippi

Ashanti read all of his information while smiling. She watched more football than basketball and chalked that up to the reason of why she probably hadn't heard of him.

"What am I doing?" she mumbled to herself and exited the browser and began scrolling through Facebook until they pulled up to Harvey's and parked. Kentay called her phone before she got out, and she took that as a sign to get Ahmad Jones out of her head.

***

Kya was almost late for registration waiting on her mom, but she finally said fuck it and went on by herself. The drive to Oxford was filled with music and memories of Kya's childhood. She couldn't depend on her mom for anything, which was why most of her time was spent at Ashanti's house. If it wasn't a new man, which was more than likely someone else's or liquor, her mom, Tisha wasn't interested. Kya never knew who her dad was. No matter how many times she asked, her mom always ignored her so she finally gave up early on as a child.

After researching thoroughly, Kya decided on attending Ole Miss because the nursing program there was phenomenal. Her mom worked as CNA, and Kya was always interested in blood, needles, and helping people so she decided nursing was a great choice for her, but vowed to be more than her mother was. Kya's mind was all over the place, but the ringing of her phone interrupted her thoughts just as she made it to campus. She talked briefly to one of her girls before parking and getting out.

The Grove was lit and Kya knew she had made the right choice of school since she liked to party so much. Ole Miss was known as one of the top three party schools. Many people flunked out, but Kya planned on partying and learning. The lines were long as hell, but two hours later, she was finally done and walking around with a few people she met viewing dorms. She couldn't afford an apartment, so a dorm would have to do. Kya told herself that she needed to find a boss nigga like Ashanti so she wouldn't have any money issues.

Kya stopped by a store after finishing up everything on campus. She went and grabbed a Strawberry Fanta and some hot chips because she was starving. While looking down and not paying attention, she bumped into someone.

"Shit… I'm sorry," Kya said embarrassed.

"It's all good lil mama. You better pay more attention though because everybody ain't as nice as me," the guy said in a flirtatious voice. When Kya finally made eye contact with him, she was mesmerized by his eyes.

"Damn!" Kya said after scanning the man who was standing in front of her from head to toe.

"Don't just stare at me… let me get your name or something," dude said to her while licking his lips.

"Kya… what's yours?" she found her voice and asked

"I'm Blow," he replied smoothly.

Kya stared at Blow and knew right away that he was boss status. They talked for a little while longer, and he paid for her items. When they walked out of the store, he asked for her cell phone, and she handed it to him without thinking twice. After dialing his number and saving his in her phone, he handed it back and headed towards a black on black Cadillac Escalade sitting on 28's. Kya knew then that her thoughts were accurate.

"Who is that bitch?" Kya heard a female voice say right as she was about to get in her car. She turned around and saw some yellow chick with bad weave standing there fussing at Blow. "Don't try to leave now. Who the fuck are you?" the girl asked, now heading towards Kya. Kya looked her up and down and couldn't help but to laugh.

"Clearly, I'm the bitch that's about to replace your busted ass," Kya snidely replied while winking at Blow.

"Don't let Blow get you fucked up," the girl forcefully replied while trying to be intimidating.

"Listen you raggedy hoe, I would advise you to get the hell away from me before I fuck you up. You don't know shit about me! I'll wipe the parking lot with your crusty ass if you don't get away from me," Kya heatedly spat while walking towards the girl. Before Kya could reach her, Blow was there and stepped between them.

"It's all good lil mama. Ima get up with you later, okay," Blow assertively said to Kya. Instead of getting into the car and leaving right away, Kya boldly walked closer to him, leaned up, and gave Blow a luscious kiss on his pretty juicy lips. Surprising the hell out of her, Blow wrapped his arms around her waist and pulled her closer to him and kissed Kya back with the same amount of vigor that she displayed. Stunned at the display unfolding right before her eyes, the girl reached around Blow, trying to sneak and throw a punch Kya's way. She missed Kya's face but landed the punch on the shoulder instead. Realizing what the fuck just happened, Kya broke the kiss and didn't waste any time turning her anger towards the ragged yellow conniving hoe. Making her connection, Kya hooked her with a right and punched the chick straight in the nose causing her to fall back, stumble, and hitting the ground hard.

Amazed my Kya's actions, Blow stood still for minute before removing her from the situation.

"Call me later Kya, "Blow smirked as he quickly ushered Kya to the car before the girl regained her balance.

Kya finally got in her car but kept her eyes focused on what was going on around her. Blow walked right past the girl and ignored her yelling and screaming behind him and hopped in his truck. Kya saw the girl kick his truck as he was pulling off, and he stopped abruptly. The girl must have known she had royally fucked up because she took off running immediately and hopped into a blue Chevy Cavalier. She didn't leave the parking lot before locking eyes with Kya again, who in returned smirked and pulled off before her. Before she left the parking lot good, Kya's cell phone rang. When she saw the word *DADDY* on the screen she smiled.

"Hey daddy!" she cooed into the phone.

"So you a lil hot head huh?" Blow said from the other end.

"Not really, but I ain't gon let nobody fuck with me and get away with it," Kya honestly replied.

"Word… I can't help but to respect that," Blow admiringly said.

"You better," Kya giggled, loving the playful banter they were establishing. Blow talked to her pretty much the whole way home, and Kya knew after the call that she was going to do anything to make him hers.

Chapter Five

The past couple of weeks had flown by, and it was already the day of Raven's baby shower. She was almost eight months pregnant and would be welcoming a little princess into the world very soon. Ashanti and Kya were at the Shrine Club putting the last touches on the decorations while talking shit to each other and catching up. College hadn't even started, and it seemed like they were already caught up in their own worlds.

"So you almost got into a fight over a nigga you had just met? You so damn crazy and some things never change huh," Ashanti said while laughing at her girl.

"Almost? Girl please... I did! Shit, I just ended it just as quickly as it begun. But hey, what can I say? She was asking for an ass whooping, and I gave her exactly what she wanted," Kya shrugged before continuing. "But, you know I been tryna stay low key lately. I got shit to prove and to accomplish, but ain't no bitch bout to check me," Kya replied while finishing up placing center pieces on the tables.

"I hear you... other than the drama, how was registration and everyone at Ole Piss?" Ashanti teasingly inquired.

"I can tell I'm going to looovvveee it there. I can't wait til you can come party with me. Oh damn, Tay ain't gon let you out like that," Kya jokingly said.

"Tay ain't my daddy," Shanti refuted while rolling her eyes. "Anyway, do you know who Ahmad Jones is?" Ashanti curiously asked her girl.

"That's the basketball player ain't it? You met him? Girl he going to the NBA soon," Kya musingly responded.

"I knew you would know. Yeah I met him on campus though," Shanti said nonchalantly.

"Why you bring him up then try to shrug it off? Biiittcchhhh let me find out you like him!" Kya perked up and said. "You know Tay really ain't shit and that would definitely be an upgrade," she joked.

"I was just asking, crazy ass girl. He is fine though," Ashanti truthfully admitted. The ringing of her phone broke up the conversation and she was very happy. Ashanti didn't want to verbalize her true thoughts and feelings to anyone because she was still confused as to why she even cared.

An hour and a half later, everything was set, and Ashanti and Kya had exactly two hours to get ready before guests were scheduled to arrive. Raven had taken it upon herself to create an event for the baby shower on Facebook and over one hundred said that they were attending. That caused an argument amongst Ashanti, Kya, and Raven because of the extra money that was going to be needed for food. Ashanti wanted to say forget the entire shower, especially with the shade that Raven had been throwing lately, but she was the type to finish things that she was dedicated to so she decided to push through. She was beyond ready to get the shower over with so that she could focus on her. Surprisingly, Kentay had been on the straight and narrow the past few weeks. Ashanti felt like he was being extra nice for some unknown reason, but she just went with the flow without overthinking.

Right on time, Ashanti and Kya finished getting dressed before the first guest arrived. They both decided to wear white halter top Chanel dresses with gold sandals and accessories to match the color scheme of the decorations. Kya's dressed hugged her 5'6 slender frame and she wished she had the curves that Ashanti possessed. Her caramel skin looked perfect under the lighting.

"Damn girl, you need to give me some of them ass and hips shit," Kya told her girl while laughing.

"You can have em shit. I can't wear half the shit I like because of these damn hips," Ashanti replied. They took pictures in the mirror while admiring each other before heading out of the bathroom.

After snapping countless pictures, the girls walked towards the front room and the place looked more like a wedding was about to take place instead of a baby shower because Ashanti went over the top with extravagant décor. Gold princess crowns, sandals, spoons, pacifiers, and cupcakes were some of the items on every table that would be used for different games. A crowd of almost sixty people were present within the first twenty minutes, but Raven still hadn't arrived. Ashanti had Kya to call her to see where she was, and Raven told her that she was on her way.

An hour later, the shower was under way, and everyone seemed to be having a good time. It ended up being about seventy people in attendance, but only about twenty of them brought gifts. That was the main reason Ashanti didn't want to do a Facebook event because she knew most people would accept the invite but only come to be nosey and eat. Raven pranced around like she was Miss America waving and smiling. There was so much tension in the room that it could be cut with a fork, and Ashanti didn't know why, so she ignored it and kept the games flowing.

When it was time for Raven to open her gifts, she went and sat in the chair that was place up front by the designated gift table after everyone was done eating. Raven opened up gift after gift until they were all gone. Even though they didn't equal in amount to the people who were present, she received gifts so big that it didn't even matter. She got a car seat, stroller, bassinet, a swing, pampers, wipes, clothes, and even a crib. Raven gave her "thank you" speech, and everyone started saying their goodbyes and leaving.

"Why don't you seem happy Raven?" Ashanti asked after pretty much everyone had left.

"Yeah, you been acting like a spoiled brat all day," Kya chimed in.

"I sent y'all pictures of which crib and car seat I wanted. I don't understand why y'all didn't get it," Raven ungratefully replied while rolling her eyes.

"You know what… we took out our money and our time and put together this nice ass shower, and you got the damn nerve to complain. We are about to go off to college while you dropped out last year to sit on your ass. Seems like someone in your position would just be grateful that we cared enough to even do this for you," Ashanti lividly fumed.

"You think you're just so much better than everyone don't you? You walk around here spending Tay's money like it's yours and always tryna upstage people. I didn't ASK you to do shit for me, you volunteered, and quite honestly, it's the least you could do," Raven angrily yelled.

"What the fuck is wrong with you Raven?" Kya asked, annoyed with her friend's behavior and attitude.

"Stay out of this Kya. I'm talking to Miss Goody Two Shoes right here. She thinks just because she was homecoming queen and made straight A's without studying, driving a Range Rover that she's the shit. Well, let me tell you something, you ain't shit, and you fell in love with an ain't shit nigga," Raven irately accused.

"Bitch, if you wasn't pregnant I would drag yo ass," Ashanti seethed stepping towards Raven.

"Wait… y'all know I ain't even the one who stop fights and shit, but what's the fucking problem Raven? We all been cool for the past couple of years and now you acting like we ain't shit," Kya pondered, wondering where in the hell all of this was coming from.

"I said this has nothing to do with you Kya," Raven screamed while keeping her eyes on Ashanti.

"You know what… I'm just bout to leave before I fuck you up and end up in jail. Call your punk ass baby daddy to help you pack up this shit," Ashanti squealed and started walking off.

"Whatever trick! Perfect timing. Looks like I don't have to call him after all. There he is walking in now," Raven coolly stated, and everyone's eyes followed the direct path that she nodded towards. Their eyes opened wide as their gazes went straight to

41

Kentay, who had just walked in and turned around to the close the door, unaware of what the hell he just stepped into.

Chapter Six

While driving down north on Montgomery Street on his way from Rock Hill where he had just finished up taking care of some business, Slick's phone started chiming with text messages through the speakers. The noise was interrupting his Kevin Gates flow, so he picked it up to see who was blowing him up. Money was on his mind twenty-four seven, and the money he had just picked up from his side hustle had him on cloud nine. Finally looking at the phone, Slick noticed that it was one of his lil jump offs blowing him up. Instead of texting back, he called since he was driving.

"Wassup," he said when she answered after the phone had only rang half a time.

"I been waiting on you to come through," Lena said from the other end of the phone. Slick thought about the constant begging she did with wanting him back on one hand, then he thought about the other things that that mouth of hers could do and told her that he was on the way.

Just a few months back, Lena meant the world to Slick. It wasn't until a video surfaced of her setting it out for the hood that Slick knew she wasn't about shit. They had been in a relationship for a year and a half, and he was thinking about putting a ring on it, but he thanked God daily that he didn't make that mistake. That made him really focus on the money and sing with the other fellas saying "these hoes ain't loyal!" Slick would never let Lena back in the way that she had been before, but it didn't stop him from fucking her and getting his nut from time to time.

Twenty minutes later, Slick was turning into Forest Creek where Lena lived. Before he could park, his phone rang again. He saw that it was Lena, ignoring her call, he parked and got out.

"Hey bae," Lena purred while opening the door before Slick could even knock.

"What up," he dryly replied and brushed by her and went and sat down on the couch. Lena closed the door and walked over to him and straddled him. She leaned down to kiss him, but he turned his head just in time to keep her lips from touching his.

"Damn Slick! How many times do I gotta say I'm sorry," Lena whined.

"Don't start that shit or I'm leaving. You already know the deal," he replied nonchalantly. Instead of responding to him, Lena made her way down to his pants and unbuttoned them, and then released his dick. "Wait, grab that condom outta my pocket and put it on," Slick told her.

"What the fuck?" Lena rasped and looked at him like he had lost his mind. Before Slick could respond to her, his phone chimed. He grabbed it and looked at his text, since Lena had copped an attitude.

Potna: It look like I'm walking into some bullshit dawg. Come meet at this baby shower shit.

"I gotta dip. You pissed off any got damn way like you don't know why I try to protect myself. I don't want my dick getting sick and shit," Slick spat and stood up. He buttoned his pants back up while Lena cussed him out. Everything went in one ear and out the other as he went and got in his Tahoe and took off wondering if the shit was really about to hit the fan.

***

"What the fuck you mean there he is now? Bitch!!" Ashanti screamed as she lunged at Raven. She punched her in the face, which caused her to fall backwards and cry out in pain. "Let me the fuck go!" Shanti yelled. By the time they let her go, Kentay had made it to the front and grabbed her, but she jerked away from him with all the force she had. Kya grabbed her and tried to calm her down.

Ashanti got away from Kya and headed towards Raven again, but a few people intervened and stopped her.

"What the hell is going on in here?" Tay questioned trying to buy some time. He pretty much knew what the deal was as he watched the scene unfold.

"Wellll… Ashanti done threw Raven here a fabulous ass baby shower, and Raven been walking around like Queen Elizabeth… thennnn she just said her baby daddy was coming to help her take her gifts home and you walked in," one of the girls who had been recording everything said all in one breath. "You wanna see the video?" she continued.

Tay made his way towards Ashanti as he watched her destroying the gifts that were in sight by opening pampers and ripping them up, throwing clothes in the punch that was left on the table, and she even demolished the remainder of the cake.

"Tay you better tell me this bitch is lying," Ashanti fumed when he made his way over to her as she continued to destroy everything that she could get her hands on.

"Calm down before you hurt my son, Shanti," Kentay told her seriously. When he made it within her personal space, Ashanti turned around and slapped the shit out of him. It surprised the both of them, especially since it was the first time Ashanti had ever put her hands on Kentay other than in a sexual way. With his high strong temper, Kentay wanted to react and bitch slap Ashanti back. However, he realized that she was feeding off of emotions after the shit Raven just confessed to her.

"I knew that shit would come back and bite me in the ass. I shouldn't have told yo ass what she was doing you sorry son of a bitch!" Raven yelled before she rapidly realized what she said. Kentay directed his attention towards Raven, and if looks could kill, she would be one dead bitch. She must have known how serious he was because she tried to clean the shit up she had just let slip while Ashanti fought to get to her. "Ashanti I'm just talking shit, but I don't care for your stuck up ass. Somebody better get my gifts to my house," Raven back paddled and walked away.

"This bitch done lost her muthafuckin mind hadn't she!?" Kya stated more than asked.

"I promise you gon' see me soon bitch!" Ashanti hollered at Raven, who in return kept walking like she didn't hear the threat.

Raven bumped into Slick while walking out of the door, and he looked at her like she was crazy but kept walking towards his boy.

"I know y'all can see that the got damn baby shower is over!" Kya irately yelled to the few remaining guests after Ashanti stormed towards the back room where they had gotten dressed at earlier.

"What the fuck happened man?" Slick asked Tay when he finally had his attention and feeling the tension that was clearly in the air.

"Man, Raven just fucked me up, and I don't know if I can fix this shit without digging a deeper hole," Kentay replied while shaking his head and rubbing his jaw.

"Got damn… you better think of a way to fix this shit," Slick spewed out.

"I can't believe that bitch did this shit," Tay said with much menace in his voice. "Take this shit to her crib fa me and let me go try to calm my girl down," Tay pleaded with Slick.

Ashanti was pissed the fuck off. She felt used, humiliated, crazy, and everything imaginable. Kya was just as shocked as Ashanti. She knew that Tay wasn't shit, but she didn't expect him to fuck around with Raven.

"That bitch is clearly jealous so just wait to see what he has to say Shanti," Kya said, trying to calm Ashanti down.

"You know how much money we spent on this damn shower… and for that bitch to front on me like that. I promise you after she has that baby her ass is mine. Ain't nothing or nobody keeping me off of her," Ashanti said calmly but firmly.

"I know girl… you know I'm hardly ever at a loss for words, but right now I am," Kya sheepishly replied. Before Ashanti could respond, Kentay walked into the room.

"Give me a minute wit my baby," he implored to Kya. Kya rolled her eyes at him, but chose to remain quiet as she exited the room.

Kentay hadn't thought of an approach by the time he walked in, but he knew that he had to get it together quick, fast, and in a hurry.

"Did you fuck her Tay?" Ashanti asked as tears started to form in her eyes. She didn't want to break down and cry, but her emotions were getting the best of her.

"She said I did baby," he cheaply replied.

"What the fuck you mean she said you did. You either did or you didn't," Ashanti said through clenched teeth.

"Let me tell you what happened baby. At Mike's bachelor party, I was fucked up. Your girl Raven was there as one of the dancers and shit. I don't remember touching her at all, but she showed me a video a couple weeks after that and apparently something happened. I still don't remember the shit, but I saw my dick in her mouth, and she said we fucked too," Kentay told Ashanti, giving her the true story of how the fling started. He knew he couldn't tell Ashanti about how he fucked Raven multiple times after that, and he hoped that she didn't ask.

Ashanti stood there staring at Tay for about five whole minutes without uttering a single word.

"It was in the past Shanti. I have been faithful since I put that ring on your finger. Please don't hold that mistake against me," Tay pleaded with her.

"Raven was supposed to be my friend Tay. This shit is fucked up," Ashanti sobbed with her tears now flowing freely down her cheeks. He made his way over to her and pulled her into his embrace.

"You see I'm being honest with you, I know it hurts, but I don't wanna lie to you," Tay affectionately told her, while leaving out the rest of the story.

"So she's the one that told you about me going to get an abortion?" Ashanti inquired as she stepped out of his embrace.

"Yeah. She texted me saying call her when I was done, and she hated that she couldn't be there. She said that she was tryna text you, but texted me so I hit her up and asked her what the hell she was talking about. She told me everything then," Tay said trying his best to make his story sound believable.

"I'm not sure I can handle this relationship if that's your baby Tay," Ashanti said quietly.

"One day at a time baby. We just gotta take it one day at a time," he replied to her and continued squeezing her tightly. "Come on, let's get outta here," Kentay said and led Ashanti out to her truck. "I'm right behind you," he told her and kissed her on the forehead before closing her door.

Chapter Seven

"I got ball!" Ahmad yelled as he took on the opponent that was coming down the court with ten seconds left on the clock. Although it was only a friendly pickup game they were playing at The Sanderson, Ahmad hated losing and his team was down by one so quite naturally, he took charge. When he saw the guy fake left and try to go right, he stripped him and headed down to the opposite end of the court where he slammed dunked the ball just before the buzzer sounded.

"Why you didn't just hold the ball nigga. Tryna be fancy and shit and made us lose," one of the guys from the other team fussed. Ahmad just laughed at them and shot a few free throws before going to grab his gym bag and leaving.

Ahmad was leaving campus with his boy Seth in the passenger seat. They were both on the basketball team at MSU. If it had not been for having to play at least two years in college, Ahmad would be in the NBA already. He didn't mind it at all because he actually wanted to obtain a degree in Physical Education, so that he could coach one day.

"Go by Sports Center so I can pick up some new socks bruh," Seth said.

"Aight… I'm hungry as fuck too, but I'll swing by there first," Ahmad replied while turning onto highway 12 leaving campus.

Traffic was a little thick since it was Friday evening, so it took Ahmad about fifteen minutes before he made it and found a parking spot at Sports Center. Seth went straight towards the Jordan socks when he walked in while Ahmad walked to the back to browse at some shoes. Out of the corner of his eye, he saw a familiar face, and he couldn't help but to smile.

"Miss beautiful, how are you?" Ahmad asked after he made his way over. He could tell that she was caught off guard, which gave him the upper hand.

"Now I come in here all the time, and I've never seen you before. When did you start working here Ashanti?" he inquired after propping his foot up on the bench that was separating the two of them.

"How did you know my name?" she asked with much curiosity.

"Well, it's right there on your name tag, but I would've already known it if you wouldn't have ran away from me on campus a few weeks back," Ahmad jokingly stated.

"Oh damn," Ashanti said, a little embarrassed. She was new to the working scene and forgot all about the name tag that she had on. After the incident with Raven and Kentay, Ashanti told herself that she needed to work to provide for her and her child and not depend on Kentay even though he hated that she got a job. "Hello Ahmad. I just started working here about a week ago," Ashanti said while blushing.

"I just love your smile," Ahmad told Ashanti while smiling himself, causing her to blush even more.

"I bet you say that to every girl you meet," Ashanti smiled and attempted to walk off, but he gently grabbed her by the arm.

"That's cute. If you wanna know if I'm single or not, just ask," he told her and laughed a little.

"I don't need to know if you're single… because I'm not," Shanti rasped.

"I peeped that hesitation. Must be trouble in paradise," Ahmad smoothly replied. He noticed the sadness that washed over Ashanti after he made that comment, so he decided to switch it up a little.

"Listen, I know someone as beautiful as you is already locked down, but I wanna be your friend. All I need is your number so that we can stay in touch. Plus since you working in one of my favorite stores, you can let me know when the shipments come in," Ahmad conceded to Ashanti, trying his best to get her number.

"I know I shouldn't even do this, but give me your number. My boyfriend is crazy as hell, but I could use a friend," Ashanti caved while pulling out her iPhone. "I'll get up with you later," Ashanti said after programming Ahmad's number in her phone and saving it as Aaliyah before walking off. She felt Ahmad staring at her, but she kept on walking to keep herself from staring right back at him.

"Who was that you was all skinning and grinning at nigga?" Seth asked as soon as they hopped back in Ahmad's truck.

"Get out my business nigga!" Ahmad laughingly speared.

"Damn it's like that? You talk about all these other hoes so why she exempt?" Seth asked while laughing.

"It's something special about her. I don't even know her man, but I'm bout to get to know her," Ahmad said while pulling out.

"If you say so. You know all these hoes look at you as a meal ticket, so don't go getting caught up and shit," Seth warned.

"It ain't even like that. She didn't even know who I was the first time we met," Ahmad informed his talkative friend.

"Still be careful man. These hoes ain't loyal," Seth honestly stated.

"I hear ya man… I hear ya," Ahmad replied and then turned the music up to drain his boy out because he knew all too well that the lecture wasn't about to be over.

***

Five minutes after Ahmad left the store, Ashanti was helping a lady find the right size shoe for her son when Kentay strolled through the door. Ashanti sighed, but she managed to muster up the fake smile that she had been wearing lately.

"What are you doing here Tay?" she asked him when he made it over to her.

"I should be asking you that question," Tay replied while looking around. "I can't believe you serious about this working shit," he continued while shaking his head.

"Don't start again Kentay. You know exactly why I'm working so don't come here and try to get me fired," Ashanti exhaled and started walking towards the customer she had been helping.

"These will work just fine. Thank you so much for your help," the lady said to Ashanti and then walked towards the front of the store to check out.

"You're welcome," Ashanti replied to her customer and then glanced at the clock on the wall and noticed that she had a little under two hours until her shift ended.

"We're going out tonight. I'll pick you up about 8:00," Kentay told Ashanti and walked out of the store. She stood there silently wishing that she wasn't so in love with him and caught up in his spell.

Later that night, while Ashanti was getting dressed, she became frustrated because all of her favorite outfits were pretty much too little. She didn't really care to go out with Tay, so that didn't help her mood, but she was going to suck it up. After trying on at least a dozen outfits, Ashanti finally settled on a black dress she had ordered online from Bebe. It was the most comfortable one she had tried on, so that's what she rolled with. When she was done with her makeup, she noticed that it was fifteen minutes until nine and Tay hadn't made it, so she called him. Kentay answered the phone after the third ring, and Ashanti heard noises in the background.

"Damn Tay, the least you could've done was told me you wasn't coming instead of standing me up," Ashanti spewed right away because she automatically knew the deal.

"I'm sorry baby. I promise Ima make it up to you. I got caught up handling this business," he pleaded with her.

"Whatever Tay," Ashanti mumbled.

"I'll be there later. Keep it wet fa me," he replied and hung up.

Ashanti vowed not to get in her feelings. She had been in her feelings too damn much lately and was blaming it on her pregnancy. Even though Tay wasn't the best man in the world, she loved him and was faithful to him, but she was tired of his shit. Picking up her phone, she shocked herself with what she did.

Aaliyah: Come and keep me company at the Chicken Shack in West Point in forty minutes if you can. No need to text back. If you can't make it I understand.

Not bothering to wait for a reply, Ashanti changed out of her dress and threw on some Rock Revival skinny jeans, a red tee shirt, and her red Converse. She could go for some catfish, hush puppies, and fries from that restaurant so whether or not Ahmad showed up, she would be okay. She couldn't dare save his name as Ahmad, and Aaliyah was the first name that popped into her head so that was what she saved it as.

Thirty minutes later, Ashanti was walking into the Chicken Shack, and the smell of the delicious food caused her stomach to growl. It was then that she realized she hadn't eaten anything since her 3:00 break at work. Before she was found a table, she spotted Ahmad and headed his way with butterflies in her stomach.

"I didn't expect you to beat me," she nervously stated as he got up to pull out her chair for her.

"Always expect the unexpected with me, beautiful," Ahmad replied while taking his seat. Ashanti blushed while getting comfortable in her seat. "I don't know what brought on our first date, but I'm happy as hell," Ahmad said while grinning.

"This isn't a date," Ashanti asserted while acknowledging in her mind that she's on a date with someone other than Kentay.

"Shittin' me! This is a date. I'm glad to know you're down to earth just like I envisioned because I love this place too," Ahmad told her.

The waitress came and took their orders, and the small talk began. It wasn't Ashanti's intentions to be so open with Ahmad, but the way he asked questions and paid so much attention to her every word had her open. She told him about her crazy relationship. However, she made it known that she would never say her boyfriend's name because she never wanted him caught up in any mess. Ahmad didn't care about the guy's name, he was just waiting on Ashanti to realize she deserved better, and he was going to make it his business to make her his. He told her that he did have a friend or two, but it was nothing serious. The way they studied each other and connected with one another was indescribable. It left both of them wanting more.

They finished their meals and were stuffed, but ordered a slice of caramel cake to share just because they weren't ready for the night to end. When the restaurant was closing, they had no choice but to leave. Ashanti was nervous about one other thing that she wanted to tell Ahmad. She felt that it would make Ahmad dismiss her with the quickness, but she felt like she owed him the truth.

"Ahmad, there's one more thing I have to tell you," Ashanti started saying while playing with the hem of her shirt.

"Aye… I don't have any kids, but I'll step up if your punk ass baby daddy don't do right," Ahmad surprised her with his words, already knowing what she was about to tell him.

"What… how…" Ashanti stuttered while looking down at the ground and shaking her head.

"Girl, I noticed the difference between the two times I saw you. I just wanna be your friend. I'm here for you and whatever happens; happens. Okay?"

"You sure you weren't sent to me as a setup? This seems too good to be true," Ashanti nervously stated.

"Only game I play is basketball baby," Ahmad replied making them both laugh. After a few more minutes of talking, they finally parted ways. Ashanti noticed that she had five missed calls from Kentay and sighed because she knew that even though he stood her up, he was going to be pissed off that she wasn't answering his calls.

"Oh fuckin' well. It is what it is," Ashanti confessed out loud to herself after pulling off and heading back towards Starkville.

Chapter Eight

"You been acting real funny lately and shit. I know you don't think I'm too dumb to notice," Kentay said as he got out of the shower and wrapped a towel around his lower body. "You even being stingy wit my pussy," he continued fussing. Ashanti just looked at him like he was crazy. It had been a month since she had started conversing with Ahmad on the regular, and she had to admit to herself that she was caught up in him. Everything between them was innocent, but she knew it wouldn't come off as innocent to Tay so she had to be extra careful with her moves. "You gon' give me some today or I gotta take it?" His question broke Ashanti from her thoughts as he put his arms around her.

"Tay, you know we have to be at the appointment in less than an hour. Don't start nothing," Ashanti whined. It would be a lie if she said she didn't want him to sex her, but she was more excited about her doctor's appointment.

"Aight, Ima let you make it right now… but that ass is mine later on," Kentay said as he walked into the closet to find something to throw on.

Twenty minutes later, they were both dressed and ready to go. Ashanti was glad that Kentay had stopped with his rants, but she knew he would get started again soon. When he was around, it had become the norm for him since Ashanti wasn't hounding him the way that she used to.

"Are you excited to find out what we're having?" Ashanti asked him after they got in the truck.

"I already know it's a boy. I don't know why you don't believe me," Kentay countered.

"I hope your feelings don't be hurt if it's a girl," Shanti reciprocated. Tay silently hoped and prayed that it was a boy because he wasn't ready to deal with two girls.

"You know you stay on that phone a lot now," Tay expressed while turning into the Women's Clinic.

"Isn't it better than nagging you about your whereabouts Kentay?" Ashanti inquired, causing him to bite his tongue and shut the hell up immediately. After parking, they got outside and went in. Ashanti filled out the required paperwork and sat back down after handing the clipboard filled with repetitive papers back to the receptionist. "Why you look so nervous?" she asked him.

"I didn't know I was," he mocked while laughing a little.

"Well, you look nervous as hell. Got me feeling like I need to be comforting you," Shanti whispered and chuckled.

"I love you, babe," Kentay confessed to Ashanti out of the blue.

'I love you too baby," Ashanti sincerely replied. Deep down, she wished that Kentay would really commit to her, and they could live happily ever after. Every time she thought that things are going great, something happened.

"Ashanti McNeal," the nurse called Ashanti's name, and she got up to head towards the back. "If you weren't going to the back with me, I could've come by myself Tay," Ashanti huffed after she noticed that he didn't get up to follow her. Kentay couldn't just sit there, so he hesitantly got up and followed behind his girl while silently praying the nurse didn't say shit about him coming to the clinic the day before with Raven. Hell, for that matter, Kentay hoped the nurse didn't open her big ass mouth period about past shit or else there would be some problems up in the doctor's office. When she recognized Kentay, the nurse narrowed her eyes and stared straight through his soul while grimacing and pouting her lips. After seeing her wide-eyed facial expression, all Tay could do was give her a death stare back with a threat in his eyes.

"Ump!" the nurse hissed when Kentay walked by and rolled her eyes.

"Let's get your height, weight, and blood pressure first," the nurse told Ashanti.

"Ugh… I know I've gained hella weight," Shanti whined.

"Well, you're pregnant sweetie, so you're supposed to. And if you've been stressed, that can cause you to gain extra weight too," the nurse tried to comfort her about her weight gain. Ashanti looked at the nurse nicely, but on the inside, she was wondering why she was acting so strange. She felt the tension between Tay and the nurse, but she remained silent. "Now that we've got that done, let's get a urine sample. Place the cup inside of the window in there when you're done, then come back out here and have a seat until your name is called again," the nurse told her sweetly.

Twenty minutes later, Ashanti was lying back on the table in a paper gown waiting for her doctor to come in. The tension started to bother Ashanti, so she confronted Kentay about it.

"The nurse that took all my vitals and shit act like she knows you, Tay. You know her?" Ashanti asked with her eyes closed. She didn't care to see his face. She just wanted to hear what he had to say.

"Nah, I don't know her like that Shanti," Tay sighed as he was relieved that the nurse didn't out him to Ashanti.

"What you mean you don't know her like that? How you know her?" Ashanti curiously inquired. Before he could answer, the doctor walked in followed by the same nurse.

"Ms. Ashanti… we're gonna go over your charts first and make sure you're on schedule with everything, and then we're gonna listen to your baby's heartbeat and see if we can get the gender since you're a little over five months. I'm happy that you decided to go through with your pregnancy," her doctor told her. When she came the last time, she was unsure of things, and she didn't follow up until now.

"I'm glad too. This baby is going to be a blessing to us," Ashanti happily announced, and the nurse went into a coughing fit.

"You okay, Gina?" Dr. Brown asked her.

"Yes Dr. Brown, I'm fine. I need to go and get some water," the nurse replied after getting herself together. Kentay nervously shifted and both Ashanti and Dr. Brown noticed.

"Let's listen to the heartbeat and see if we can get the gender why don't we," the doctor said and then rubbed the cold jelly onto Shanti's stomach causing her to jump. Moments later, a sound that was similar to a horse galloping could be heard throughout the room.

"He or she sounds as strong as an Ox," Dr. Brown said while chuckling with the Doppler still in his hand. "He or she has his legs shut tight, so we won't be able to tell the gender today. Maybe next time," he told them after pointing to the ultra sound machine and printing off sonograms for them and talking for a few more minutes. "You went a long time without prenatal care, but everything looks just fine. Just keep doing what you're doing, and we will have a healthy baby in a little over four months," Dr. Brown said as he helped Ashanti sit up. "Any questions?" he asked. Ashanti told him no while shaking her head. "In that case, I'll see you back in about six weeks," he told her and left the room.

When Ashanti stood to get dressed, Kentay told her that he was going to find the bathroom. She was too excited to question him as she stared at the sonogram. Kentay strolled down the hall and back towards the front. He was pushed into a room before turning the corner, and he already knew what the deal was.

"So, you made me get an abortion while two other bitches having your baby. Does Miss Ashanti know that you were just up here with Raven yesterday?" the nurse vibrantly screamed at him while folding her arms across her chest, causing her breasts to push up. Instead of replying to her right away, Kentay unbuckled his pants and pulled his dick out.

"I know this what you want. Go on and suck me off and shut the fuck up," he finally told her after pulling his dick completely out. Without hesitation, she dropped down on her knees and filled her mouth with the dick that she craved so much. "Suck that shit good. I know you miss him so make up for lost time," Tay coaxed her. He began fucking her mouth and a few minutes later, his cum was going down her throat. "If you even think about starting some shit, I'll make yo ass disappear. Now fix yourself up and get back to work. I'll call you when I call you," Kentay threatened after gathering himself and preparing to exit.

Opening the door and making sure the coast is clear, Tay eased out of the door and headed back towards Ashanti's room. Seeing her fully dressed, he went over and gave her a hard kiss on the lips. Kentay wanted to go deeper, but he knew once he did, Ashanti would be giving up the pussy sooner rather than later. Instead, he grabbed her by the hands and proceeded to leave the doctor's office.

"Where are we going?" Ashanti asked when she noticed that they weren't headed towards her condo.

"We going to celebrate babe," Kentay cheerfully answered back as they headed towards highways 82 and exited on the ramp to go east. The conversation flowed freely between both of them since Ashanti decided to brush everything under the rug. "I know I fuck up at times, but I really do love you, and I want us to work," Kentay admitted to her.

"I love you too. I know I nag a lot, so I'm gonna try to do better. You just gotta stop doing stupid shit," Ashanti scolded him while trying her best to keep her anger in check. "Where we going anyway?" she asked again feeling a little annoyed and irritated.

"To feed yo ass because you starving my baby. The only time you can tell yo ass is pregnant is if you naked or got on super tight clothes. You starving my baby trying not to gain weight and shit," Tay told her while speaking nothing but the truth. Ashanti opened her mouth to get smart with him, but she closed it right back because deep down she was loving the fact that he cared about her and the baby.

"I can't believe a baby is growing inside of me," she exclaimed after a few moments of silence.

"Well believe it. I hope you have him before your due date. A Christmas baby will be the shit," Kentay spiritedly stated.

"The due date is January 18th. You pushing it Tay," Ashanti fussed with angst in her voice.

"You right, you right," Kentay said while exiting off on Highway 45. When he made that turn, it finally clicked where he was headed.

"What you wanna name the baby?" Ashanti inquired.

"Shit, he gon be a junior. Fuck you think?" Tay boldly stated.

"Nigga you swear. Might get your initials, but ion even like your name," Ashanti laughed.

"Don't play wit me. That's KJ in there cooking and you betta know it," Kentay lovingly and optimistically boasted.

"I hear ya talking," Ashanti responded and laughed.

When Kentay turned into the Chicken Shack, deep down, Ashanti felt some type of way. The only thing she could think about was the time she had spent there with Ahmad. The smile that was on her face could have lit up ten Christmas trees, and Tay didn't miss it.

"You haven't been here in a while I know, so I decided to bring you on over," he spoke with a smile plastered on his face. As soon as he put the truck in park, his phone rang. He looked at the caller ID and sighed. A few seconds after he silenced it, it rang again, so he just powered it off. "I'll handle that business later. Let's go, babe," he told Shanti and opened the door. During the entire meal, Ahmad was on Ashanti's mind, and she couldn't help but wonder if she was as guilty of cheating as Tay was.

Chapter Nine

"How often Ima get this pussy when you go off to college?" Slick asked Kya while he had her bent over the back of the couch at his apartment. Normally, he never entertained his women at his place, but when Kya hit him up asking for the dick and gave him her location, he said what the hell and gave her the address. There hadn't been a woman there since he kicked Lena out, and he planned on keeping it that way for a little while longer. Actually, his mind was all on his money.

"Whenever you come and get it daddy!" Kya cried out to him while throwing her ass back at him as if her life depended on it. She loved the curve of his dick, and she knew that she was going to miss it but getting her feelings caught up in Slick was out of the question, so Kya knew how to play her position. The money he broke her off with from time to time was an added bonus because the sex was already A1.

After a few more strokes, Slick roughly turned Kya around and threw her leg over his shoulder and glided knee deep in the pussy.

"Ahhh… oh shit!" Kya joyously screamed.

"You know you like this rough shit girl," he told her and the only thing she could do was moan because he wasn't telling nothing but the truth. "Shit girl!" Slick squawked after Kya squeezed her pelvic muscles tight around his dick. Several strokes later, Slick finally filled the magnum condom up with his cum and went and flushed it down the toilet. He always told himself it was better to be safe than sorry.

Kya went and washed up in the bathroom and when she came back out, she got a good look at his place.

"This a nice place you got here. Where yo woman at because I know yo ass didn't decorate this by yourself," Kya mentioned while touching an exquisite piece of art on the wall.

"I live alone nosey ass and why I can't have taste?" Slick asked while popping open a Heineken.

"Hmph. I'm just saying but I ain't gon argue wit ya," Kya said while smirking. "Anyways, thanks for the dick," Kya mused and headed towards the door.

Before she could turn the knob, someone started beating on the door like a maniac.

"Yo, what the fuck?" Slick yelled while heading towards the door. Kya, being who she was, opened the door and Lena fell forward because she lost her balance when the door swung open.

"I knew you had another bitch. Is this who you been ignoring me for? This bitch right here?" Lena confronted Slick while looking Kya up and down.

"How the fuck did you get through the gate?" Slick bellowed, annoyed with Lena's trifling ways. He lived in a complex down South Montgomery where you had to get by a guard to come through. Slick was puzzled as fuck as to how Lena could have gotten by.

"This hoe prolly sucked off the guard," Kya snapped back while laughing and not knowing how true her statement was. The comment angered Lena more than she already was so she swung on Kya, hitting her in the left jaw. "You bitch!" Kya screamed and jumped on Lena, hitting her repeatedly. When Slick finally pulled her up, Kya kicked Lena as much as she could while continuing with her threats. "Nah let me go. This bitch wanna run up and shit. Ima show her ass who not to fuck wit. Dumb hoe," Kya barked trying her best to get out of Slick's grasp to avail.

Lena wanted to scream back, but she wasn't able to do so with her blood filled mouth. Slick carried Kya outside and told her to call him later, because he needed to handle some business but not before handing her a stack.

"I knew yo ass had a woman. Better be glad I don't give a fuck," Kya hissed after she gathered herself and walked off. She went and hopped in her Honda and headed out. With only two more weeks until it was time to leave for school, Kya decided that it was time to go ahead and grab the last few items she needed for her dorm. She prayed that she didn't have a fucked up roommate since she wasn't as fortunate enough to get an apartment her freshman year like Ashanti.

On the ride to Wal-Mart, Kya listened to one of her cousins who was a local rapper that had mad talent. She couldn't wait for Varus Bell to blow up. She had just finished listening to Lucky LaDon Luciano, another local who was the shit. Riding down highway 12, Kya told herself she couldn't wait to get to school so that she could party like never before. Starkville wasn't known to be a party city. They forever had new restaurants popping up, which should make it easy for people to get jobs, but Kya was ready for the real nightlife.

"Damn I need to wash my car, but it's packed as hell out there," Kya said as she passed Mr. Bubbles.

Wal-Mart was packed when Kya made it and she ended up parking damn near at the gas pumps.

"Ugh… I hate coming to this damn place," she mumbled to herself after finally turning the car off and grabbing her purse. Kya went to her notes on her phone and pulled up her school list in hopes that it would keep her on track with only getting necessary items. She knew that it was highly unlikely, but it was worth a try. After being in the crowded ass store for only about fifteen minutes, she heard a familiar voice and looked up. "Well, heeey Miss Raven," Kya seethed and headed towards her. She hadn't seen her since the baby shower and Raven had been ignoring her calls, so running into her was a good thing so that she could try to find out what the problem was.

"Oh, hey Kya," Raven dryly replied.

"Bitch, don't be all dry with me. If you weren't pregnant, I would really whoop yo ass," Kya seriously told her.

"I don't have time for this bullshit," Raven exhaustedly refuted and tried to walk away, but Kya grabbed her by the arm.

"Nah, you gon talk to me!" Kya heatedly spat. "I've been calling and texting you tryna figure out what the hell been going on and you ain't replied yet. You know Shanti was the one who spent the majority on your baby shower and that's how you repay her. What the fuck is wrong with you?" Kya continued ranting.

"Kya, I hate that you're in the middle of this, but this doesn't concern you. Ashanti and I aren't besties just like y'all aren't either. We just kick it together and besides, Tay loves me and we are going to be together when our son is born," Raven snappishly replied and walked off.

"So you choosing dick over a friend?" Kya asked with a frown on her face, trying to make senses of the situation.

"I just said that we all aren't really friends, but if that's the way you wanna look at it, I'm choosing some bomb ass dick over everything," Raven turned around and said, and then walked away without a care in the world. In one of Kya's rare moments, she stood there discombobulated for a few moments until she finally snapped out of her daze and continued with her shopping. She needed to get the hell out of Wal-Mart and hit Slick up for round two of the day. She planned on sucking and fucking him dry for the next couple of weeks until she left for college.

Chapter Ten

"Hold on Tay. I'm tired as shit!" Ashanti fussed while trying to keep up with him while rushing through the airport. It seemed like she was growing every day since going to her doctor's appointment and her baby bump was showing vividly.

"We supposed to been here an hour ago. Come on baby, we almost there," Tay said while continuing to pull both suitcases behind him and prompting Ashanti to keep up with him. They were bypassing security at the Memphis International Airport, but still had ways to go to board the private jet that was waiting on them. Kentay had paid one of his partners to use his jet to take Ashanti on a surprise trip. Since he had been fucking up, Kentay figured that it was the least he could do before she started school. She didn't want to miss work, but he had someone write her a doctor's excuse for a few days off so that her job wouldn't be in jeopardy.

After finally getting on the jet and taking their seats, Kentay immediately ordered a double shot of Hennessy on the rocks. Ashanti settled for some ginger ale.

"Now where are we going? You still ain't gon tell me?" Shanti asked while getting comfortable.

"It's a surprise ma. I keep telling you that," Tay told her while laughing.

"Ugh… you can still tell me and I'll act surprised," Ashanti said while poking her lips out.

"Nah… I'll just wait and let you see. Now let me handle this last business before we take off. Get comfortable," Kentay told her before pulling his iPhone out to call and Tay to make sure everything was lined up according to plan.

Kentay hung up the phone after handling business, and as soon as Ashanti heard him wrapping his call up, she started ending her text conversation.

"Tell Aaliyah you busy for the next few days," Kentay said catching Ashanti off guard.

"Whatever," she said and rolled her eyes, keeping her cool. Ashanti put a piece of gum in her mouth right after they were told that they were about to take off. Sometimes her ears popped, and sometimes they didn't but she always chewed gum to be on the safe side. It had been almost a year since Kentay had taken her on a trip. She had to lie to her mom the last time, but to her, it was all worth it. Ashanti hoped that this trip would put them all the way back on track and told herself that she would stop communicating with Ahmad if it did. In her mind, it was harmless anyway, but she knew that things had the potential to get deep at the right moment.

When Ashanti felt someone nudging her, she woke up from her sleep to find Kentay staring at her. After a few moments, he held up the postcard that had Anantara The Palm Dubai Resort on it.

"Oh, myyy gawwddd!! Are you serious? Is that where we going?" Ashanti squealed.

"Anything for you, my love. I know you think I don't be listening, but I do. You glad to be away from that lil job of yours now ain't ya," Tay replied.

"I'm gonna let that lil shade you throwing slide so we can enjoy Dubai. Thank you so much, baby," Ashanti said and leaned over and kissed him.

"We have about thirty minutes before we descend into our destination," the pilot said.

"You wanna join the mile high club with our last few minutes?" Tay smirked and started rubbing his hands up Ashanti's thighs. The look of seduction she gave him made his dick harder than it already was.

***

"That's how you start off a trip!" Tay said after they hopped into the awaiting limo that was parked by the curb when they walked outside. Ashanti couldn't do anything but smile with the way Tay had just worked her over in seven minutes tops. She came three times and was already looking forward to the rest of the trip because she knew it would only get better. The driver pulled up at their resort thirty minutes later, and it looked exactly like the postcard. Ashanti was in awe of the beauty. She instantly took out her phone and started posting videos on Snap Chat. The water was the prettiest blue that Ashanti had ever seen in person, and the resort was on the water with trees strategically placed between each villa.

"I'm not gonna want go home," Ashanti squealed into the camera and then turned it on Kentay.

As soon as they got settled in their spot, Tay went out on the patio and rolled a blunt. Ashanti busied herself with pulling her clothes out so that she could find something to wear to dinner later that night. She pulled out a pink dress she had ordered online from Charlotte Russe and some nude color wedges. When she was done figuring out what she was going to wear, Ashanti laid down on the bed and drifted off to sleep.

"Umm… wait… we can't. I'm pregnant," Ashanti mumbled when she felt her panties being removed. Seconds later, his fingers slipped into her already wet mound.

"Ain't no stopping! This my pussy and it's hot and wet, ready for me!" she heard the sexy voice reply as he continued to finger her. Moments later, his mouth replaced his hands, and he went to work on her pearl.

It was feeling so good that Ashanti tried to run because she knew it was wrong, but he kept pulling her back towards him.

"Oh, my gawd!! Ahh…" Ashanti's orgasm cut off her words and caused her to finally open her eyes. When she saw Tay getting ready to enter her, she quickly realized that she was only dreaming about Ahmad.

"What's wrong wit you?" Kentay asked when he noticed the crazed look on her face.

"Nothing... ain't no way you not gon let me return the favor right quick tho!" Ashanti said after thinking of the best way to divert Kentay's mind back to sex. It worked because he stopped just as he put the tip in and laid flat on his back.

Ashanti maneuvered herself up and around and positioned herself to take Kentay's long, hard, and thick dick into her mouth. It had been a minute since she had given him head because of their issues, but she figured he deserved it at the moment since she was laying there thinking about another man while he was pleasuring her. He loved it when she spit on his dick, so she stopped sucking, spit on it, and then licked it all back up seductively.

"Shit baby! You know what I like," he moaned, pumping her up. Ashanti went to work on his dick and found herself enjoying it more than he was. She sucked, licked, and massaged his shaft to perfection. She knew he was getting ready to cum by the tenseness in his body, but he pulled her up to keep from exploding, flipped her over, and entered her from the back.

He slid his eight and a half inches into her with ease because she was wetter than the Pacific Ocean.

"Oh, shit baby... this shit wet as fuck!" Tay rasped as he continued to deep stroke her. Ashanti couldn't reply if she wanted to. Her head was deep in the pillow as she threw her ass back at Kentay as much as she could. He loved hitting it from the back. It was a mixture of pleasure and pain for her, more pleasure than anything, but she was always happy when he was done because that was one position she always lost in. A few moments later, Kentay grunted and filled her up with enough cum to make quadruplets, then flopped down on the bed beside her. "Damn that was good. That shit was extra wet baby. Wetter than it's ever been. You musta been having a wet dream," Kentay mulled and pulled Shanti closer to him.

"Actually I was, and you were right on time," she replied sexily with her eyes closed.

"Ima need fa you to keep dreaming like that," he told her and smacked her on the ass. Ashanti snuggled closer to him but didn't open her mouth to reply.

Later that night, Tay surprised Ashanti with a new outfit so she wore it as it complimented the white Armani linen suit he wore. They both looked angelic in their all white as they left and headed for dinner at one of the five-star restaurants near the resort. The hostess greeted promptly upon arrival and smiled at both of them. Ashanti was too caught up in the beauty of the place to notice the way the hostess was staring at Tay. They were led to a table that had a magnificent view of the water. The chandeliers, artwork, and overall atmosphere of the restaurant were absolutely amazing.

After only being seated for a few minutes, the waitress came and took their drink orders, along with appetizers and entrees. Kentay reached across the table and grabbed Ashanti's hand and rubbed it.

"I know you hate me at times baby, but please don't leave me. You've been rocking wit me and I appreciate it, no doubt. I know you tired of hearing the same ole shit, but I mean it. We bout to be… nah scratch that, we already a family. I hate that job you got, but I understand why you got it so I ain't trippin'. You just gotta make sure you taking care of my son," Tay told her while looking directly in her eyes. Ashanti felt herself becoming emotional as he talked because all she ever wanted was for him to love her unconditionally and be committed to her and only her.

"Do you think that Raven's baby is yours? That's gonna be a tough pill to swallow. Just the thought makes me cringe," Ashanti finally said after a few moments of silence.

"I don't think so, but there's a chance. I don't wanna talk about her right now, though," Kentay replied after choosing his words carefully. He knew that Raven should have been the least of Ashanti's worries, but there was no way that he could tell her that. He just hoped and prayed that Courtney never popped back up. Kentay could tell that Ashanti wanted to say more, but he was happy as hell when she changed the subject and started talking about baby names. The waitress had eased their food in front of them, and they started eating right away.

"So what names do you have in mind?" Ashanti asked him while rubbing her protruding belly.

"What kinda question is that? He gon be a junior. The fuck!" Kentay replied while with his mouth full.

"Ugh… we gonna have to compromise on the name baby," Ashanti said.

"Nah… ain't no compromising that. What dad don't name their son after them?" Tay asked and took a sip of his drink.

"Next topic," Ashanti laughed. He knew that she always teased him about his name so there was no need to elaborate on why she didn't want to name her child after him.

After finishing up with their food, they headed to take a walk on the beach. They ditched their shoes and walked barefoot in the sand. The sand between their toes felt good and as they walked, the sounds of birds chirping could be heard, along with the fresh smell of water.

"This is still only day one, and I feel like this is the best trip we've ever taken," Ashanti said as she intertwined her fingers between Tay's.

"You just wait until tomorrow. I've got a full day lined up for you," he told her.

"You know I'm not with you for your money or anything right?" Ashanti asked him.

"Of course I know that. That's why I fuck wit you the long way. You deserve everything I do for you. You gon be my wife eventually girl," Kentay replied.

"I can't wait!" Ashanti excitedly responded. She knew right then and there that she couldn't continue talking to Ahmad because it was only going to complicate things more. If Kentay was finally ready and willing to do right, she felt like she had to stay by his side because she had invested so much time into him. Kentay picked her up and spun her around causing her to scream with excitement.

After they finished playing around with each other, Kentay led Ashanti to a beach chair that he spotted and laid her down. As he kissed her body, the only sounds that could be heard were the sounds of the water and Ashanti's moaning.

"Oh my gawd, Tay… baby! You bout to make me cum with just your touch," Ashanti panted. Instead of Kentay answering her, he just continued using his skillful tongue to make her body succumb to him. He knew without a doubt that Ashanti was the woman of any man's dream, and he needed to do right by her, but he couldn't help but think with his dick at times, all the time. As soon as he slid his fingers over her clit and massaged it, Ashanti came instantly. Lowering his head even further, Kentay sucked up all of her juices and ate her until she released again in his mouth. His dick was hard as a rock, but he didn't want to penetrate her. He wanted her to feel like it was all about her.

The next day, Ashanti was catered to again starting very early in the morning with breakfast in bed. The French toast, bacon, eggs, sausage, and strawberries with whipped cream were delicious. After she finished eating and getting dressed, Kentay took her to the Spa, where she got the full-service treatment that lasted almost five hours. She thought that he was going to leave her there, but he surprised her by staying and actually joining in with getting a massage. Once they finally finished, they were both relaxed and ready to lay down, but Kentay wanted to take her shopping and to dinner, because he knew the finger foods that had were about to wear off. They were scheduled to leave the next day at noon, so he had to make the best of the last night. After shopping until they couldn't shop anymore, they ended up going back to the room and ordering take-out from a nearby restaurant that was highly recommended. They spent the remainder of their time with enjoying each other with no interruptions. Both of their phones had been turned off upon arrival. When it was time to leave the next day,

Ashanti wasn't ready to go at all, but school was about to start in a few days, and she knew she needed to prepare herself.

"Thanks for an awesome trip baby. I loved it, but not as much as I love you," Ashanti told Kentay the next day when they were buckled in and ready for take-off.

"You're welcome babe. I'll do anything for you. Believe that!" he told her and leaned over and kissed her. They both slept the entire flight. When they landed back in Memphis, they departed the private jet and headed to their car. Kentay finally turned his phone on, and the text messages came flooding in, making his blood boil. He replied to Slick telling him that he would arrive in two hours, knowing that he was almost three hours away. Shit, Kentay meant every word of his text because he was not the one to be fucked with.

Chapter Eleven

After that episode with Lena popping up at his house, Slick made sure to go and check the security at his complex. He didn't want to get rough with the people where he rested his head, but that shit was unacceptable to him. Any little slip up could cost him his freedom, and he knew that if Lena could manipulate them then anyone could. It had him thinking about going ahead and buying a house out in a secluded area. He had hooked up with Kya one time since then, but they both agreed that they needed to end their little rendezvous, especially since she was about to leave. The understanding that they had with each other was one the duo claim they could handle, but they really couldn't. Slick was definitely going to miss Kya and her fire pussy but told himself that everything was all good.

Outside of the drug world, Slick fought dogs and made a shit load of money. He actually made more doing that, but he had to be extra careful because he knew the white people would throw the book at you for fucking with animals. Shiiid, that was proven with Michael Vick. Since Tay was out of town, Slick was on his way to the trap out in Blackjack. He hardly ever went out to that one, but Kentay had him checking on every spot just to be on the safe side. While riding and listening to Future, Slick was extra hype for a party that was happening at Club Kiss later that night. It was one of the homie's birthdays and pretty much everybody would be in Crawford that night.

Slick made it to his destination almost thirty minutes later and got an eerie feeling as soon as he pulled up. He immediately surveyed his surroundings. Taking the safety off of both Sig Sauer P250 that he had on him, Slick exited his truck while paying extra attention to his surroundings. Instead of going through the front door, he eased around back and quietly slipped in.

"Hurry the fuck up so we can get outta here man," Slick heard a voice harshly whisper.

"That nigga out in Rock Hill," another voice affirmed. That voice sounded familiar to Slick. He was glad that he decided to ease in the back entrance because he was about to catch some thieving ass niggas off guard. It was hard to hear a car pull up from the back of the trap, but only an amateur would forget that while being grimy.

After cautiously easing closer, Slick stood beside the refrigerator until he heard the footsteps becoming nearer.

"Wait, I forgot to push that picture all the way back," the voice said in a rushing manner.

"Nigga I'll be outside waiting. You gon' get us killed," the other guy uttered with cautious in his voice.

"Nah nigga, you done got yo self muthafuckin' killed," Slick said through clenched teeth as he stared Twan in the face.

"I… I can… I can explain," Twan, one of their runners, said while stuttering.

"Explain what nigga? Why you got two duffle bags on yo got damn shoulders that are more than likely filled with product or money? Huh, is that what you trying to explain. Or, are you trying to explain why the fuck you and your boy thought you could steal from us," Slick gritted while pointing the gun in Twan's face.

POP!

When he saw Twan try to move, Slick fired off one shot to his dome. Twan was dead before he hit the dirty ass floor of the trap house. Slick checked for the other voice that he had previously heard but was met with silence. Suddenly, Slick heard movement towards the back and took off running in search of the other guy. He didn't immediately recognize the soon-to-be-dead muthafucka's voice, so he needed to get to him ASAP.

By the time Slick made it to the back room where the product was, the room was empty, the window was open, and the curtains were blowing.

"Fuck!" Slick shouted while looking out and not seeing a soul. Slick hopped out of the window in search of the other guy but came up empty-handed. "Dammit!! Shit!! I'm so glad that I brought my ass down here to check on this shit. These muthafuckers feeling brave as fuck, thinking that while Tay is away, shit won't get checked. They got the game fucked up. I know one muthafuckin' thang…whoever this son of a bitch is, his ass is mine when we finally cross paths," Slick declared with much venom. He cursed to himself as he looked around the area more before heading back inside. Once he made it to the kitchen, Slick looked down at Twan's lifeless body and wondered why in the fuck he would be stealing from the team. His gut was telling him that it had to be done by force because Twan had been loyal for a little over two years now. While thinking, he sent a text to the cleanup crew as well sent an urgent text to Kentay. He knew that Tay was scheduled to be back in town soon, but he never expected him to have to come back to bullshit.

***

Three hours later, the trap house was clean, and Slick was looking for Kentay to pull up at any moment. Just when he was about to pull his phone out of his pocket, it chimed with a text from one of the partners. Slick didn't bother replying back because he heard Tay pulling up out front.

"Nigga it was an accident right before I got off 55 or I woulda made it sooner. What the fuck happened?" Kentay sharply asked when Slick met him outside. Slick ran down everything that happened and also filled Tay in on his thoughts about what he thought happened. "Da hell? Mane, these mofo's don't know the shit they just stepped in. I'm 'bout to make sure they know shit stank. These bitches fixin' to see just how froggy my muthafuckin' ass can jump. So on the real, it's at least one more bitch ass nigga that gotta die along with whoever sent their trifling asses, huh!" Tay furiously stated while rubbing his hands on his chin and thinking.

"Hell yeah and I'm bout to be on a full mission starting right fuckin' now," Slick hotly replied.

Not believing the shit that just went down, Kentay wondered who had the biggest balls to come after his shit.

"What pussy ass muthafuckas decided to try me?" Tay fumed while pacing the floor after they went inside. He walked towards the kitchen to check things out for himself. He couldn't leave anything to chance and had to put eyes on the cleanup himself. As expected, there wasn't a trace of the murder. "The cleanup crew is the shit. Gotta give them a helluva bonus this year," Kentay conceded to himself while checking out everything and not finding one spot or blemish.

"Whoever it is… they just signed their death wish," Slick announced as he walked into the kitchen and opened the fridge. He popped the top on a Corona and downed it in less than thirty seconds. "You best believe that shit," he continued saying after throwing the bottle in the garbage can.

***

Slick was riding through the hood with Kentay on the passenger side scoping out the scene. They had rolled up on the crew in Black Jack and then rode out to Rock Hill to see what the streets were talking bout. Tay was smoking on a blunt to relax his mind. They hadn't had any real issues other than the trap house dilemma, but he wasn't naive enough to know that there was always someone somewhere plotting twenty-four seven. After riding around for damn near two hours, the partnas still didn't have any solid leads. They decided to still go to the party at Club Kiss later that night to see if the streets would be talking.

Lucky for them, the bags that Twan had held the most cash and product so whoever was with him only got about two or three bricks. Kentay could easily replace that loss, but that wasn't the point. In his eyes, no one could cross him and live to tell the story.

Later that night, Kentay was at Ashanti's condo getting dressed. He hadn't officially moved in, but he had as much shit there as he did at his place. Tay made it a habit of staying with her as much as possible to try and strengthen their relationship. Eventually, he told himself that they would build a house together and make everything official. But for the moment, Tay still needed his own space for more than one reason. Ashanti was out with a girl named Aaliyah that she met while she was at the bookstore, so Kentay sent her a text letting her know that he was headed out.

Dressed in black Balmain jeans, a black shirt, and his black Timbs, Tay checked himself in the mirror while putting on his watch and necklace. After spraying on some Versace Eros Eau De, he grabbed his phone and dipped out. Noticing that it was just fifteen minutes until eleven, he knew that he was right on schedule. Tay was pretty sure that Slick was already there scoping out shit. Tay trusted him so all was well in his eyes. Tay hopped in his truck, still blasting Kevin Gates from earlier. Not bothering to change anything, he backed out and headed towards Crawford.

As soon as he turned on Oktoc road, his phone rang.

"Got dammit," he screamed when he noticed that it was Raven calling. "This bitch getting outta hand," he said before finally answering the second call since he sent the first one to voicemail. "What the fuck you want Raven?" Tay answered not bothering with a formal greeting.

"Why the fuck you been ignoring me? Hell, I didn't make this baby by my damn self," Raven replied with an attitude, matching his voice intensity.

"Look, I don't know why you be tripping and shit. You already know the deal so stop tryna make shit more than it is. Plus, I already told you after we get a blood test, Ima do what the fuck I gotta do, but we ain't gon be together. Get that shit through your fuckin' head," Tay said as nice as he could. It took everything in him not to cuss her the fuck out. However, Tay knew that he was partially responsible for the situation they were in, so he couldn't completely blame her. Giving her the dick so freely like he was doing had her head gone.

"You just act like I ain't shit. Was I only a fuck to you? All those times?" she asked with a voice full of pity and hurt.

"Raven, don't do this aight!" Kentay replied becoming annoyed.

"If Ashanti wasn't in the picture, you would want me wouldn't you?" Raven questioned him.

"Who knows? You could be right but she here, and she ain't going nowhere so cut the shit. Now I'm busy. I'll holla at ya later," Tay replied thinking that he had just said the best thing to get through Raven's head.

"Call me lat…" Raven started saying but Kentay didn't hear her because he had already hung up.

When he pulled up at the club, cars were lined up all up and down the road, and the parking lot was packed.

"Fuck. I ain't parking my shit all the way back here," Kentay said to himself. He decided to go ahead and drive up close to the front and just when he turned in, a car was pulling out of its spot. He turned his music down and backed into it. Before he could get out of his truck, Tay heard some niggas that appeared to be arguing, but he couldn't tell if it was just a drunken argument or if it was something serious.

POP! POP! POP! POP!

"What the fuck? Are they shooting at me? Are they targeting me or am I just collateral damage," Kentay fumed while ducking down when his window was shattered. He didn't have time to look up to see who was blasting, and he didn't wanna take the chance either and get popped. Tay cranked his truck back up and sped out of the parking lot. He heard screams and felt a bump, but he didn't give a fuck who or what it was. "Man, fuck this shit! Sorry to whoever or whatever I just hit. Shouldn't have your ass in my fuckin' way," Tay spoke out loud to himself while getting the hell out of dodge. He commanded Siri to call Slick, and he hoped his homie was straight. Tay drove up the highway going full speed ahead. He hoped his shattered window would stay in place until he got to his destination.

Chapter Twelve

Two Weeks Later…

It was August 18th, the first official day of class and Ashanti was also a couple of weeks from being five months pregnant. She had a belly but she wasn't fat or out of shape. She refused to let herself get that way because she already had ass and hips for days. Sitting in her Range while parked in the commuter east zone, Ashanti pulled her MAC lip gloss out of purse and freshened up her lips. Her lips were a blessing and a curse. A blessing because she loved how full and perfect they were and knew what they could do, but a curse because of the disrespectful ass comments niggas made about them.

After making sure that everything was all good, Ashanti got out and headed towards Lee Hall where her English Composition class was held.

"What's up luscious lips?" a voice called from behind Ashanti while she was walking across the yard. Normally, she would be mad, but she couldn't get mad at that voice.

"Hey Ahmad. What you doing here?" Ashanti asked when he made it beside her.

"I walked over here to see you before class," Ahmad specified as his reasoning for being near Lee Hall.

"But your class is all the way on the other side of campus. You gon' be late," Shanti considerately explained.

"Ion care nun bout that girl. I wanted to see you and check on my God baby," Ahmad told her with a big ass grin on his face.

Ashanti couldn't do anything but blush. She had every intention on breaking the friendship that she had developed with Ahmad off, but he wouldn't allow it. Even after meeting up with him after getting back from Dubai face to face, she still couldn't get through to him. Looking into his eyes, she couldn't help but smile. Ahmad was dressed in a MSU tee shirt, Nike basketball shorts and some Nike slides. It wouldn't be him if a basketball wasn't in his hand.

"You're just too much," Ashanti finally said while laughing.

"You got a break after your second class right? Meet me in the Union so we can grab something to eat," Ahmad directed and walked off before she could turn him down. Ashanti walked on to class, deep down she was ready to meet him again already.

After finishing up English and Chemistry classes, Ashanti pulled her iPhone out to call Kya, but Ahmad walked up on her before she knew it. She forgot all about hitting the call button. She hadn't talked to Kya in a couple of weeks, and it seemed as if they were already drifting apart before school even got started good, which was something they vowed not to do.

"I was gonna meet you there," Ashanti told Ahmad after he grabbed her bag while they walked towards the union.

"I didn't wanna take any chances of you dipping out on me. I been out here waiting since my class ended thirty minutes ago," he told her.

"You're just too much," Ashanti replied.

They made it to the Union and decided to grab something to eat from Chick Fil'A. Ashanti felt her phone vibrating and pulled it out of her pocket. She sighed when she noticed it was Kentay but decided to answer anyway.

"Yes," she dryly answered. She hadn't seen him in two days and now he was calling like everything was all good. "Fine," Ashanti replied, continuing to give Kentay one word answers. "No... okay... yeah," she said and finally hung up. Throwing her phone into her purse, she tried to shift her mood back to where it was before, but it was hard for her to do.

"Wanna talk about it?" Ahmad asked her.

"Not really. I can't bore you with my mess of a life," Ashanti insisted.

"What do you think friends are for? Go on and get it off your chest," he prompted her.

"I just don't know about this relationship I'm in. One minute I love him, the next minute I hate him. I'm only eighteen and I have a condo and Range Rover, thanks to him. Going to school for free, and he always keeps money in my pockets, even though I started working. I don't want for shit, but I feel empty on the inside most days. I feel like my baby deserves to be raised with both parents, and I just hope Tay really steps up when that time comes. I know I'm not perfect either, look at me sitting here venting to another man that I'm attracted..." Ashanti vented but cut the last part of her sentence off when she felt like she had said too much.

"You called out all that material stuff ma but that doesn't replace real love. I ain't even gon' lie, I'm feeling you something serious, and I wanna be your friend. But, if I ever get the opportunity to treat you like the queen you are, you gon' forget all about that clown ass nigga you wit. I ain't got no lil babies or nothing, so I can't tell you how to feel about wanting to be wit ya baby daddy, but I will say this... if you ain't happy already, a child ain't gon' fix it, and you gotta be happy for your baby to be happy. I know all about dysfunctional families and shit. My moms and pops argued day in and day out. He slept on the couch most nights. They tried to make it work for me and my sister, but little did they know, we woulda been happy as hell if they woulda both went their separate ways. That shit was miserable as hell, looking at them coexist. They split up after I left for school, and I was happy for them. Life is too short to live in misery. But I'm glad you attracted to me," Ahmad finished up by saying and smiling.

Ashanti sat there taking all of his words in and really taking them to heart. Every single word that he spoke, she knew all of it was nothing but the truth, but she still felt like she just couldn't leave Tay.

"You got practice today?" Ashanti changed the subject and asked Ahmad.

"Yep… in a couple of hours," he replied.

"Heeyyy Ahmad! I can't wait to see you play," a girl stopped and said as she walked by the table. She smirked at Ashanti and walked off.

"See… you got all these damn groupies and I would be ready to kick some ass if you was my man for real," Ashanti told him.

"You know I ain't been nothing but straight up wit you. I do got a few lil dips, but if you was mine, you wouldn't have to worry bout none of that bullshit. I'm single and free to mingle, unless you ready to lock me down," he replied trying to see what she would say.

"Hmph… you sure I wouldn't be going from one player to another?" she asked after taking a sip of her lemonade.

"I'm a ball player baby… that's it," Ahmad told her.

"If you say so… I can't wait to see you play though," Ashanti happily replied. They finished their food and Ahmad walked Ashanti to her next class, which was in Carpenter Hall. They talked freely to each other until they made it. There was an awkward silence before she walked into her class. Ashanti was feeling like she was supposed to kiss Ahmad, but she couldn't move. He smirked at her, gave her a hug, and then headed towards Coliseum.

Chapter Thirteen

"Girl, you better get up. You already missed two days of class this week," Kya told her roommate, Amanda.

"Ugh… these classes easy as fuck, but I'm bout to get up. But, I don't see how you be so damn energetic off of a couple hours of sleep," Amanda groaned. She finally pulled herself from the bed and headed for the shower. Kya and Amanda had been out partying every single night since they moved into their dorm. Whoever said that a party goes on at Oxford every night wasn't lying at all because the options were endless. Kya couldn't wait to go out later, but she planned on kicking it with Blow instead of Amanda.

"I'll see ya later," Kya called out to Amanda before leaving out of the room.

Kya drank her Red Bull while she was on her way to her Anatomy and Physiology class. Science was one of her favorite subjects, and it came to her naturally. However, she still needed to be alert because all of her classes were set to build on each other. Kya planned on becoming a Registered Nurse in two years, which was why she was doubling up on classes. After working for a couple of years, she had plans to become a Nurse Practitioner. "Have fun but stay focused!" Kya told herself while dropping her can in the trash and walking inside of the building.

Classes went by fast as hell, and Kya found herself going through her closet pulling out a couple of outfits to throw in her overnight bag. Things with Blow had been flowing smoothly, but they hadn't had sex yet, but in Kya's eyes, it was time. She was ready to throw her pussy on him to see exactly what he was working with. Hell, she wanted to ensure she wasn't wasting her time. Good sex was important to her. Blow had been free with his money and time, but he was stingy with his dick.

"Ima find out what that nigga working wit soon," Kya said as she threw the last of her garments in her bag.

Later that night after eating at Burger King with Amanda, Blow rolled up and scooped Kya up. She left her car on campus since he told her that he was picking her up. She assumed that they were going to party again, but he told her that he wanted her to take a ride with him. Kya didn't complain, she just kicked back and relaxed, so that she could enjoy the ride.

"Where we going anyway?" she asked after Blow finally got off of the phone.

"Just sit back and ride baby," he smoothly replied.

"I'm tryna figure out why you ain't tried to fuck yet!? I'm horny as shit, so I hope you be ready tonight!" Kya bluntly told Blow.

"Lil hot ass. I'm trying not to turn you out yet. Once you get this bomb dick, you gon' be all mine. Ima have yo ass climbing walls and shit tryna get away from me," Blow said while laughing.

"I hope you ain't just talkin' shit nigga. I heard about niggas that talk mad shit and can't fuck worth a lick," Kya teased and tried to ease over and grab Blow's dick, but he swatted her hand away.

"Don't try to touch this pole yet ma… you gon' feel it soon enough. We got some other business to take care of first," Blow playfully told her. "Roll me up one," he demanded to Kya, and she complied because she could use a hit herself.

After smoking the blunt and realizing that they were headed to Memphis, Kya leaned back, closed her eyes, and took a nap. It wasn't until the truck stopped abruptly and scuffling was heard that Kya woke up. She noticed Blow had someone hemmed up and threw him in the trunk. Everything was happening so fast that Kya's head started to spin.

"What the fuck you doing?" she screamed at Blow once he got back in the car and took off. The look he gave her let her know to shut the fuck up right away. Kya was never scared of shit, but she also wasn't dumb either. She began to feel like taking the ride with Blow was the biggest mistake ever.

About forty-five minutes later, Blow turned down a dark alley and parked. The bumping in the trunk got louder once he killed the engine to his car.

"Get out!" Blow demanded.

"What the fuck you mean 'get out'? Nigga, I ain't getting outta this car in the middle of nowhere. You got me fuc..." Kya's words were cut short when Blow backhanded her.

"Get outta the got damn car," he told her through gritted teeth. Kya reluctantly got out of the car and walked towards the back where Blow had already walked to. When he held a gun out for her to grab, her heart dropped and her knees buckled. All kinds of thoughts were running through her mind. Kya opened her mouth to talk, but no words came out.

"Here! When I open this trunk, shoot that mu'fucka in the head," Blow sternly stated. Kya's eyes bucked. She had done a lot of shit in her days, but killing wasn't on the list.

"Are you fuckin' serious?" she asked him dumbfounded.

"As a muthafuckin' heart attack!" he simply replied.

When Kya didn't take the gun fast enough, Blow shoved it in her hands and pulled another one out of his pocket and aimed it at her head.

"Now, when I open this trunk, you better blast off or that's gon' be yo ass. You understand?" Blow inquired. Kya shook her head yes while trying to figure out what in the fuck she had gotten herself into. The crazed look Blow had in his eyes was one she hadn't see in them before. She was scared shitless on the inside but showed no fear on the outside. "Aight, here we go. Shoot when I drag him out," Blow said and Kya pointed the gun towards the trunk. She didn't want to kill anyone, but she didn't want to die either, so when Blow opened the trunk and yanked the man out, she pulled the trigger and shot him in the chest. "Shoot him again," Blow demanded. The next bullet landed in his leg while Blow blasted off one to his dome. "Let's go," he told her. Kya was too frozen to move, so Blow pushed her to the car and practically threw her in.

She didn't realize that she was still holding the gun until Blow took it out of her hands when he stopped at a store twenty minutes later.

"Now, what just happened back there... nobody knows about it but me and you. As long as you stay in line, we'll keep it that way. You too pretty to go to jail," Blow told her. When he got out to pump some gas, Kya thought about calling Amanda... or Ashanti, but she couldn't will herself to move. She could only sit there and think about how Blow had just blackmailed her, and she knew that he had more bullshit in store. She could feel it in her bones.

"Fuccckkk! Fuck, fuck, fuck, fuck, fuck!!" Kya mumbled under her breath. She was pissed because she hadn't gotten caught up in any bullshit that she didn't see coming in a long time.

For the first time ever, Kya felt stuck. In her mind, something was strongly telling and pleading with her that she needed to keep her smart mouth in check before it cost her, her life. When Blow got back in the car, he handed her some swishers, a Coke, and a bag of hot Cheetos.

"So, you ready to see what this big dick feel like?" Blow asked nonchalantly while pulling back on the highway and chuckling. He acted like they hadn't just kill someone. Hell, she couldn't tell you what the dude looked like, but she had just participated in murder by force.

Might as well get a good fuck after this bullshit Kya thought to herself. Well, I hope it's a good fuck. Nawl fuck that shit! It better be a got damn good fuck.

"Hell yeah, I'm ready," she finally replied as she turned her head and gave him a fake smile. Fuck a damn Coke! I need some Crown or Paul Masson right fucking now. This shit is for the fucking birds man, she mused to herself as she turned her face towards the passenger's side window, looking at nothing in particular. Blow turned the music up and kept driving.

Thirty minutes later, they pulled up at a Holiday Inn Express. Kya assumed they were about to head back to Oxford, but she was cool with getting a room. She didn't have much of a choice since she wasn't driving so decided to just make the best of it. Blow gave her some money to go and check in, and she noticed that he pulled some powder out of his pocket.

"What the fuck?" she mumbled to herself while slamming the door and heading inside with her overnight bag and purse. When everything was set, she sent Blow a text with the room number and decided to go and hop in the shower. Looking down, Kya realized that she had small spots of blood on her. "Fuck. I hope nobody noticed this shit," she nervously stated.

After drying off, Kya wrapped the towel around her body and walked out of the bathroom. Blow was standing by the window talking on the phone, but he hung up after she walked towards him. Not wasting any time, Kya tugged at his pants, but he swatted her hands away.

"Let me taste that pussy first girl," he told her.

"You ain't said nothin but a word," Kya eagerly replied and dropped the towel, exposing her slim, firm, and blemish free body. Dropping down to his knees, Blow dove head first into her mound. Kya's juices began to flow like a river. He was feasting on her like it was his last meal. Kya found herself fucking Blow's face, and it seemed to make him more aggressive. "Oh shit! I'm bout to cum. Eat this pussy baby," Kya coaxed him. She loved giving head, but she was a sucker for it herself, so at the moment, all was well in her eyes.

Thirty minutes and four orgasms later, Blow was sucking on Kya's pussy, but she was ready for some dick at that point.

"Let me feel that dick baby," she told him through her moans and trying to sit up. Blow didn't allow her to sit up.

"I got you girl… lay back and relax," he told her. When he reached in his pants pockets and pulled a Magnum condom out,

Kya's pussy started to pulsate. Her heart sank when he stepped out of his pants and boxers, and she saw what he was working with.

What in the whole fuck?! Kya wanted to scream out loud, but instead she willed herself to only say it in her head. She was looking at a dick that was equivalent to the size of a newborn baby. *Where in the fuck is he gon' put that condom? I know damn well this gotta be a joke. What in the motherfuck?* Kya had thoughts racing through her head at a mile per minute.

"You ready girl?" Blow asked while lifting Kya's legs over her head. She couldn't find the words to answer. The next thing she knew, Blow was talking mad shit, but she didn't feel a muthafuckin' thing. She laid there in pure disgust trying to wake herself up from the nightmare that she was having. Less than ninety seconds later, Blow let out the loudest growl that Kya had ever heard from a human saying he was about to cum. "Got damn! You got some good pussy. I'm glad I got this shit on lock!" Blow said after he got up and headed towards the bathroom.

"Fuck my life!" Kya angrily screamed and pulled the pillow over her head.

Chapter Fourteen

"I'm sick of that bitch. Why can't she just see that Tay loves me and leave him the fuck alone? We gonna be a family whether she wants it or not. As soon as I have this baby, he won't be able to leave me alone," Raven said to herself while pacing back and forth across her living room floor and rubbing her big belly. Being due any day now, Raven was ready to drop the load and get her figure and her man back. He hadn't sexed her in the past two months, but as soon as Raven had the baby, she had plans for him knowing that he couldn't resist her head game. Raven had been trying her best to figure out a way to get rid of Ashanti without getting herself in any trouble, and she hoped that the plan she currently had in motion would work out the way she envisioned it.

"Arrgghhh!!" Raven screamed and doubled over in pain after a sharp pain pierced through her stomach. She read online that taking some castor oil would make her go into labor, and she had drank almost half of the bottle she purchased but didn't expect anything to happen so soon. As soon as Raven stood up, another pain hit her causing her to double over in pain again. After a few minutes, Raven eased to the end table and picked up her cell phone. She placed a call to Kentay, but he didn't answer. Pains were now shooting through her back to back to back, so she grabbed her car keys and headed for the door. She was thankful that her overnight bag was already packed and in her car, but things weren't going according to her plan. She wanted Kentay to be the one to take her to the hospital, not driving herself.

Raven wasn't expecting the pain to be as bad as it was. Actually, she had been spending all of her time plotting on how to get rid of Ashanti and not preparing for her baby at all. The only things that she had were the gifts that were given to her at her baby shower. Raven headed towards Oktibbeha County Hospital. At the moment, she was happy that she decided not to have her baby in Columbus because she was sure that she wouldn't have been able to make that drive by herself with the way she was currently feeling.

After stopping one time, swerving a few times, and cursing repeatedly, Raven pulled up the hospital fifteen minutes later. She almost hit a man, but when she opened the door, he noticed the condition that she was in and ran to get some help.

A nurse ran out with a wheelchair less than two minutes later. Right before Raven was ushered into the chair, she felt water gushing down her legs and began to panic.

"Oh shit… oh shit!" Raven panicked.

"Just calm down. Your water just broke but you're in the right place," the nurse said while helping Raven sit down and pushing her inside. Raven was taken straight up to the fourth floor where Labor and Delivery was. The nurse asked her if she had someone that they could call and Raven hurriedly gave her Kentay's number. She knew calling him from her phone wouldn't help, so she hoped if he received a call from the hospital he would come right away.

"Just tell him that he's listed as next of kin, and he needs to come right away," Raven cried to the nurse.

***

"How's school and everything going?" Kentay asked Ashanti when she walked in from class and work. "You look tired as hell," he continued talking before she had a chance to reply.

"It's going okay. I'm surprised to see you here," Ashanti said after she threw her purse and bag down on the couch.

"Shit been mad crazy lately, but I wanna take you out tonight," Tay told her.

"I'm going to the basketball game tonight. It's the season opener," Shanti snappily replied.

"Men or women?" Tay inquired.

"Men, they're playing Alabama," Ashanti told him.

"I didn't even know you liked basketball," he said while eyeing her closely.

"I'm a freshman in college Tay. I wanna do different stuff and still enjoy even if I'm not staying on campus. You wanna go?" she asked, trying to make it seem like she was just going to be going, offering for him to go but knowing he would decline.

"You know what… yeah I'll roll out there. It's a cat that I need to see ball on the college level but never found the time. What time it start?" Tay asked her.

"It's at seven," Ashanti replied. She was pissed off on the inside, but she couldn't let it show on the outside and take the chance of Kentay questioning her. Knowing how she acted when she was always in Ahmad's presence, Ashanti silently prayed that something would pop up to keep him from going with her.

"Cool. I'll be ready," Kentay said and walked up to Ashanti and rubbed on her belly. 'How my son doing? Lil Junior," he asked her.

"Here you go with that," she replied while giggling. "The baby is fine. Next doctor appointment is in a couple of weeks," Shanti told him.

"Good. Now let me go and get fresh so we can roll out in a few," Tay told her and headed for the bedroom. "Yo, go check out the other room too," he called out to her.

Ashanti headed towards the other bedroom, which was going to be the baby's room and was in awe when she got to the door.

"Oh my God!" she said as tears started running down her face when she noticed everything that Tay had done. Ashanti walked over to the crib and admired its beauty while playing with the mobile. When she touched it, music started playing, and it caught her off guard. "Daddy has hooked you up already so you better be a boy," Ashanti said while rubbing her stomach. Everything in the room was white, blue, and yellow, including the bedding and curtains. Huggies pampers and wipes lined the walls that ranged from sizes newborn all the way up to five. A high chair, stroller, walker, bassinet, bouncer, changing table, car seat, and all other types of baby items filled the room. Noticing that the closet door was open, Ashanti walked towards it and was floored even more. It was filled with more pampers and clothes and shoes for three babies.

When Ashanti walked out of the closet, Tay was standing there smiling.

"Baby… when…why… damn you bought everything," Ashanti said while hugging him tightly.

"I know I fuck up from time to time, but y'all won't ever have to worry bout shit. That's on my life, I got y'all," Kentay told her.

"I don't even need a baby shower," Ashanti said more to herself than to him.

"Fuck a baby shower. It don't be filled with nothing but nosey, jealous, hating ass bitches," Tay replied.

"You do have a point I guess," Ashanti slightly agreed. However, she wouldn't mind her friends and family getting together and celebrating her baby with her.

Fifteen minutes later after Ashanti had changed into more comfortable clothes, they were ready to head to the Hump for the basketball game. Ashanti began to feel a little bad about not wanting Kentay to go at first after seeing everything that he had done, but she still didn't want to be in the same room at the same time with him and Ahmad. Her plans to stay after the game and to congratulate Ahmad were ruined, but she told herself that she would make it up to him. Kentay's phone rang as soon as he put his hand on the knob. It was an unidentified number, but he answered anyway. After hearing what the nurse at the hospital said, he knew that it was Raven. She had been calling and texting him nonstop, but he ignored her, assuming she was just crying out for attention.

"Babe... some shit just popped up, and Ima have to handle it. I'll drop you off at the game and come back as soon as I get it situated," Kentay told Ashanti.

"Aww babe. I was looking forward to hanging out with you," Ashanti halfway lied.

"I know, but Ima make it up to you. I promise," he told her. "Come on. I'll run you out there," Tay continued.

"You go on and handle your business. I can drive," Ashanti told him.

"You sure?" he inquired.

"Yeah, I ain't handicap Tay," Shanti said while laughing.

"I'll call you in a few babe," Kentay said and gave her a kiss on her pretty little luscious lips before heading out the door and leading Ashanti to her truck where he rubbed her belly and kissed her again.

"I love you babe!" he told her.

"I love you too," she replied while silently thanking God for answering her prayer.

***

When Kentay made it to the hospital, he headed straight to the fourth floor after inquiring about Labor and Delivery. He was asked to sign in and get a visitor's pass, but he ignored the request of the little old white lady and headed straight for the elevator. After he made it up, there was a lot of commotion going on with beeping taking over the intercom. Kentay finally made it to someone that could help him, and they pointed him in the direction of the nursery. As soon as he laid eyes on the third baby, he knew without a doubt that it was his little girl.

"Damn," he said to himself, but his heart began to melt a little as he admired her beauty.

"Are you with the family of this precious baby girl?" a nurse asked, snapping Kentay out of his trance.

"Uhh… yeah" he answered after clearing his throat.

"Well the mom had to be rushed into surgery. You may wanna go and check on her," the nurse told him.

"She ain't my… What the hell happened?" Kentay asked after catching himself.

"I don't know what all went wrong. They had to resuscitate her, and I'm sure it won't be a good idea for her to be alone once she's placed in a room," the nurse told him. "You can head down to the desk at the opposite end to find out more. Congrats on your little beauty," the nurse told him and walked off.

Two hours later, Raven was finally placed in a room, but she was heavily sedated and appeared to be dead to the world. Kentay found out that she had to have an emergency C-Section due to not dilating past two after her water broke. During the C-Section, she went into shock and began losing excessive amounts of blood. Kentay was told that Raven wouldn't be discharged for at least a week, but the baby would be discharged in two days. After Raven's discharge, she would need help with everything. He sat there in awe as he stared at her wondering how in the hell he was going to be able to handle the situation that was placed before him.

Chapter Fifteen

"Yayyy! I'm so proud of you. You played great!" Ashanti told Ahmad as soon as he made his way to her after leaving the locker room.

"You my good luck charm!" he told her while smiling and pulling her in for a hug.

"You really were in a zone out there. I can tell that you really love the game. Everything looked so natural to you," Shanti told him in admiration.

"I do love it. Basketball was my escape, but I told you that you my good luck charm, so Ima need you at all my games," Ahmad told her while staring into her eyes. He couldn't help but to lick his bottom lip after his eyes landed on her luscious lips. All he could think about was how bad he wanted to kiss them and to taste them, but he didn't want to disrespect her so he changed the subject. "So you wanna go somewhere and celebrate with me? Please?" he asked her while pouting a little.

"I would love to," Ashanti replied. She briefly thought about Kentay, but he hadn't called or texted since he disappeared, so she thought what the hell and walked off with Ahmad.

Being one of the star basketball players at Mississippi State came with perks around town. Since it was late, all of the decent restaurants were closed or were about to close, but Ahmad put in a call to the chef he knew at The Veranda, and he opened up just for him. He had a taste for steak and they made the best in town, so that's where he was headed to with Ashanti trailing behind him. They made it to the restaurant in less than ten minutes since it was close to campus. Ahmad must have told the chef that the dinner was special because when they walked in, Ashanti followed him to a table near the back that had candles and red rose petals on it. In the middle of the table was a bucket of ice with a bottle of Sparkling White Grape Juice inside.

"Oh wow! How did you pull all of this off so fast?" Ashanti said after Ahmad helped her into her seat. "Let me find out you had this planned for someone else," she said as he sat down.

"I order Domino's for my jump offs girl," he told her and chuckled.

"You so full of shit," Ashanti replied while laughing.

"I'm just being honest baby. I ain't never been on a real date with none of these females up here, and they never seemed to care," he replied while filling both of their wine glasses with juice.

"Were those your parents you were talking to after the game?" Ashanti inquired.

"Yep. I started to let them meet their future daughter in law, but I didn't wanna scare you off," he replied and chuckled.

"They seem to be getting along great tonight. I guess you were right when you said they are better apart," Ashanti stated.

"Yeah, they are definitely better apart. My mom found out my pops had a baby before her that he never told her about, but they was together at the time. That started all of their arguments," Ahmad retorted.

"So you have an older sibling? Have you ever met them?" Ashanti asked.

"Nah I never met him. I guess since they were tryna make the marriage work, my dad never brought him around. I heard him say that when he tried to connect with him, it didn't go well, so I guess that's why too. I mean, I wouldn't respect a nigga that wasn't there for me either," Ahmad replied.

"Well, that sounds like a touchy subject, but if you got a brother out there somewhere, I do hope that you can meet him and get to know him for yourself," Ashanti replied.

Before Ahmad could respond, the chef came and sat their food down in front of them. The steaks, loaded baked potatoes, asparagus, and homemade rolls looked mouthwatering. Ahmad surprised Ashanti by reaching across the table, grabbing her hands, and saying grace. When he finished, they dived into their meals and continued talking while eating. It was after midnight before they finished up and parted ways. It was getting harder and harder for both of them to keep hiding their true feelings.

Chapter Sixteen

"I still can't believe muthafuckin Twan had to go down like that!" Slick said to his boy Dro, who was riding in the passenger seat of his truck with the seat leaned all the way back.

"I can't believe that shit either yo. Like what kinda fuck shit was he on?" Dro said while shaking his head.

"That shit is a mystery. You still ain't heard shit in the streets?" Slick asked him.

"Not a word dawg. You know when I hear anything, you and Tay gon' know too," Dro replied.

"Where that nigga Tay at anyway? And which one of y'all took the nigga Twan out? The streets saying it's Tay," Dro stated.

"Tay taking care of some business. And that other shit is irrelevant bruh," Slick countered.

They were on highway 45 headed back from Macon where they had met up with some cats about a little business. Normally, Slick would be riding by himself when handling shit, but he made it his business to take at least one of the homies with him, so that he could make sure their vibes were still on point with everything. It was becoming a headache not knowing who else was involved with Twan. There had been many sleepless nights and probably many more to come. By the time they made it back to Starkville, it was almost ten o'clock and Slick was starving. After he dropped Dro off at his girl's house in Chandler Park, Slick headed to Wing Stop and grabbed some lemon pepper wings with fries and headed to the crib.

As soon as Slick finished eating, his phone chimed with a text message. He picked it up and read the message from Tay.

Tay: Dawg, this bitch done had the baby.

Slick: Well congrats nigga! I guess!

Tay: *It's damn shol my baby, but I got a mu'fuckin problem bruh.*

Slick: *What now nigga?*

Tay: *The hoe almost died during delivery or some shit. Bunch of problems and she gon be in this bitch a week, but the baby get out in two days.*

Slick: *Got damn bruh. What the fuck you gon do?*

Tay: *Hell if I know. I ain't even told Shanti nothing yet.*

Slick: *You know this gon break her dawg. You better figure out what you gon do. Where Shanti at now?*

Tay: *Basketball game. Ima need yo help, but I'll holla at you tomorrow.*

Slick: *Aight, bet.*

When Slick got done texting Tay, his phone rang before he even had time to process the entire situation his boy was in. After noticing that it was Lena, he let it go to voicemail because he didn't have time for her drama at the moment. He told himself that he was really gonna have to stop fucking Lena because she acted like that they were back together when they weren't.

"Damn, never thought I would say I missed Kya's lil hot ass because that was some good no strings attached fucking. Ima let her be though," Slick said before throwing his phone and letting the TV watch him.

***

After Kentay finished up texting his boy, he turned towards the mobile bassinet where the baby was sleeping and just stared. It felt like his heart was pulling in a hundred different directions. He never meant to fuck up and get Raven pregnant, but he knew Ashanti wouldn't be able to handle the news of the baby really being his. Admitting to her that he did sleep with her friend was one thing, but to have a baby was a whole different ball game. He couldn't walk around knowing that a child was his and not take care of it either, so he had some serious decisions to make. Raven had yet to wake up, but the doctors assured him that it was normal and nothing to worry about at the moment.

"Damn man… I can't believe I let this shit happen," Kentay said to himself. He closed his eyes to think when his phone began to vibrate. Feeling like shit for the situation he was in, he sighed and let Ashanti's call go to voicemail telling himself that he would deal with it later, but not at the moment.

***

"Are you following me?" Ashanti asked Ahmad while laughing a little when he answered the phone.

"You making it sound like I'm a stalker girl. I'm just making sure you safe until you make your turn," he told her.

They had just left the Veranda and Ashanti couldn't help but to smile at the thoughts of the wonderful time they had. Noticing that Ahmad was following her, she decided to use it as an excuse to call him. They made small talk until she made the turn, and then she hung up but not before telling him that she would text him as soon as she made it inside. Ashanti wanted to keep talking to him, but she didn't want to take the chance of Kentay being in the living room when she walked in and having to cut her conversation short.

After parking in her designated space, Ashanti grabbed her purse, threw her phone in it and got out. Hitting the alarm on her truck, she headed to her condo. An eerie feeling washed over her, but she shrugged it off and kept walking. When she didn't see Tay's truck, she wondered if he was going to make it back that night. As soon as Ashanti unlocked the door, someone grabbed her around her mouth and put a gun to her head.

"Don't fuckin" scream! Just take me to the money and the bricks, and I'll let you live," a man harshly stated. Ashanti began to shake and her knees buckled. The tight grip he had on her mouth, she couldn't scream if she wanted to. "Let's go bitch! I know it's some shit in this nice ass place," the man commanded and pushed her inside.

Tears were flowing freely down Ashanti's cheeks at that point. The words Kentay spoke to her popped vividly into her head.

"I know ain't no pussy ass niggas bold enough pop up where my family rest their heads, but in these streets, you gotta be prepared for any muthafuckin thang. So if anybody get crazy and come here, you just stay calm and lead em to the picture of the Obama family. It's a safe behind it. Cooperate, stay calm and give em everything inside," Kentay's words rang in her head. Ashanti willed herself to keep moving forward while being pushed from behind, until she made it to the picture. No one would know there was a safe behind that picture just by looking. It took Kentay's street smarts to make that happen.

When Ashanti finally opened the safe, the guy pushed her to the side and grabbed the three bricks that were inside as well as four bands of money.

"Now do I have to kill you? Get your got damn ass on the fucking floor. Now!" the man spat at her after he put the bricks and the money in the bag he was carrying.

"Please… please don't!" Ashanti sobbed really hard while placing her hands protectively on her stomach.

"Don't get up off the floor until after you count to five hundred," he said and slapped her in the nose with the barrel of the gun before running full speed out the door. Blood gushed out of Ashanti's nose and the pain was excruciating. She held her cries in as best as she could because she wasn't ready to die.

After she felt like the coast was clear, Ashanti reached into her purse and grabbed her phone and called Kentay. When he didn't answer, she became frustrated and was about to hit redial, but the phone rang and stopped her. Ashanti slid the button and cried into the phone uncontrollably.

"Calm down! What's wrong…? I'm outside, tell me what number you're in," Ahmad said from the other end of the phone. Ashanti sobbed but he understood that she said she was in G4. A few minutes later, Ahmad rushed inside and found Ashanti still on the floor crying.

"What happened? I turned around once you never texted because I felt like something was wrong," Ahmad said while bending down and pulling Ashanti up. When he looked at her face, he went into beast mode, a side Ashanti hadn't witnessed before. "What the fuck happened? Who did this shit? If you say that punk ass nigga of yours did this, you leaving here tonight!" Ahmad fumed.

Ashanti finally calmed down and was able to talk. Ahmad went and got a towel and cleaned her face up and made her an ice patch. When she explained what happened, the next question he asked was where her man was. Ashanti didn't have any idea, so Ahmad made her get up and told her that he was taking her to the emergency room to make sure that everything was okay with her and the baby. She insisted that she was fine, but he wasn't taking no for an answer, so she finally obliged. Having thoughts of calling Kentay back, she quickly dismissed them after realizing he hadn't called her back yet. Calling the cops was out of the question because she knew what type of life her man lived, and the police were always the enemy.

They made it to the hospital ten minutes later and Ahmad pulled around to emergency. He double parked and ran inside to get someone to come and help Ashanti. The whole ride there, Ashanti continued to plead with him that she was fine, but he ignored her. When he told her to sit back, relax, and let him be a man, she finally remained quiet. It was evident that he cared for her at that very moment. She knew it before but that was confirmation to her. A nurse came outside with a wheelchair and forced Ashanti to sit down and proceeded to take her inside. The emergency room wasn't packed, so a different nurse gathered all of Ashanti's vitals immediately. Her blood pressure was 142/88. They told her that was a little elevated, but explained to her that it was probably because of what happened. Everything else seemed to be fine, including the baby. However, the doctor said that he wasn't going to clear her to leave until her blood pressure dropped and they would check again within an hour.

"You want anything to snack on while we wait?" Ahmad asked Ashanti.

"Hmm… I could eat a snack. Maybe some Cheetos," she told him.

"Make those baked Cheetos. We have them in the vending machine, but it's upstairs. I went all the way up to the fourth floor to grab some because the machine is out of them down here," the nurse replied.

"You don't have to go all the way up there," Ashanti stated softly.

"I got this. You just relax," Ahmad said and left.

"You know, you're really blessed to have him. You better be good to him young lady." the nurse told Ashanti and walked out.

Ahmad made it up to the fourth floor and found the vending machine. He grabbed a Gatorade for himself and a bottle of water along with the Cheetos for Ashanti and turned to leave.

"My bad dawg," Ahmad said after he bumped into someone.

"Shit that's on me. I wasn't even paying attention," the man replied. "Aye… Ahmad Jones right? I was supposed to come and see you play tonight, but I got caught up here. You keep ballin out there youngsta. You going places," the guy told him.

"I appreciate that homie. Ball is all I know," Ahmad joyfully stated. The man wanted to say more, but instead, he dapped Ahmad up and told him that he would be sure to catch him on the court soon. They parted ways after a few more moments.

Chapter Seventeen

"Maannn fuck this shit!" Kentay said and got up to leave the hospital. It was almost three o'clock in the morning, and he knew that Ashanti was going to be pissed off because he didn't answer her call or call her back.

"Where you going?" Raven asked in a groggy voice.

"Bout time you woke up. I'm bout to dip out," Kentay told her.

"You coming back right? We just had a baby you know," Raven whined.

"Yeah… I gotta handle some shit, but I'll be back," Kentay told her and left. Raven smiled and drifted back off to sleep. He went and peeked in on the baby in the nursery, and then headed out.

Kentay thought about not going to his crib, but decided that he might as well get the argument over with Ashanti and move forward. He knew that he could easily tell her that he was handling street shit but hadn't figured out how or when to tell her about Raven having the baby. Using his key, Tay unlocked the door and walked inside. Before he made it to the bedroom, he noticed the picture of the Obama family wasn't in place. Reaching for his gun, he cursed when he realized he didn't have it on him since he had just left the hospital. Ashanti must have heard him because she appeared right before him with a butcher knife in one hand and a bat in the other.

"Oh… it's just you this time. You finally decided to show up," Ashanti said while rolling her eyes and turning to head back towards the bedroom.

"What the fuck happened here?" Kentay fumed after noticing her callous reaction.

"If you would have answered your fucking phone or at least had the decency to call back, then you would know someone put a got damn gun to my head, threatened, and robbed me," Ashanti shouted as tears that she tried so hard to fight back began pouring down her cheeks. It was at that point when Kentay noticed Ashanti's swollen face. He was pissed the fuck off on the inside, but the only thing he did was go to Ashanti and pulled her into his embrace.

"I'm so sorry baby. I'm supposed to always protect you and I wasn't here. I fucked up, and I'll spend the rest of my life making it up to you. I don't know what I would do if… I can't believe some nigga even tried me like this," Kentay poured his heart out to Ashanti. For the first time ever, he cried along with her and then led her to the bed where he held her until she fell asleep. He didn't sleep one wink, the only thing on his mind was revenge.

Around 8:30 when Ashanti began to stir, Kentay pulled her closer to him and began rubbing on her. His hands eased down from her belly to her throbbing pussy. Even though she was pissed at him, she couldn't control the way her body reacted to him. Before she could turn over fully on her back, Kentay had ripped her panties off and was feasting on her. The way he was eating her, you would've thought he was trying to eat enough to last him a week. When he bit and nibbled on Ashanti's clit, her first orgasm took over her body, and she began to squirt all over the place.

"That's right! Let them juices flow for daddy!" Kentay coaxed her. It was like her body couldn't help but to succumb to his voice and commands because orgasms started hitting her back to back.

Ashanti was so drained that she couldn't do anything but lay there as Tay entered into her slowly. She moaned and called his name over and over as he slid in and out of her with ease. His dick was covered with her juices, and it turned him on to look down at it.

"This my pussy baby. My name on it. Look how it grips this big ass dick," Tay told her as he continued making love to her. "Whose pussy is it?" Kentay asked her.

"Yours… it's yours baby!" Ashanti panted. Tay stopped and lifted Ashanti's gown all the way over her head and exposed her perky breasts. Her nipples were standing at attention and waiting on him, so he bent down and sucked, licked, and bit them in rotations just the way he knew Ashanti loved it. When she squeezed her pelvic muscles around his shaft, he eased back and up and stroked her slowly while applying pressure to her clitoris.

"Whose pussy is this again?" he asked her.

"Ohhh shit… it's all yours! Fuck me Tay! Please!" Ashanti cried.

That was all Kentay needed to hear. He began deep stroking Ashanti, causing her legs to shake.

"Oh my gawd… you feel so good," Ashanti screamed as he hit her spot back to back to back.

"Got damn… I'm bout to cum baby," Kentay grunted. Just when Ashanti thought that she didn't have any more cum to give, she came right along with him. When he was done, he got up and went to the bathroom and fixed a warm towel, and then came back and cleaned Ashanti up before washing himself up. Ashanti couldn't move even if she wanted to.

Thirty minutes later, Kentay walked back in the room carrying a plate of French toast, bacon, scrambled eggs, and a glass of orange juice.

"Damn… you got me scared as shit baby. I get the best sex ever and breakfast in bed. What did you do?" Ashanti asked after he sat the plate in her lap.

"Eat up baby. We'll discuss it in a few, but you know I gotta go handle this business," Kentay said and left out of the room before he had to further explain himself.

***

Raven had forgotten all about her phone until it started ringing from the other side of the room. She couldn't move, but thankfully a nurse walked in to check on her as soon as it stopped ringing, and Raven asked her to grab it out of her bag for her. When the nurse picked up the phone, it started ringing again so she hurriedly handed it to Raven.

"Shit!" Raven said when she noticed that it was her boyfriend Jason calling. He was out of town working, but she knew that he was about to be pissed that he wasn't around when she went into labor. If he had known that she was really already nine months, he would've never gone back to work after his last run, but Raven had convinced him otherwise.

"Hey Jason. I was just about to call you and let you know what happened," Raven weakly stated.

"What's wrong?" Jason asked in a voice full of concern. After Raven told him that she went into labor a little early, he told her that he was on the way. He was a cross country truck driver, but he was only in Texas, so he told her to give him eight hours and he would be there. Raven tried to tell him not to worry. However, the anger in his voice made her shut the fuck up because Jason wasn't the type to be mean or violent so it scared her. The only thing she could do was tell him okay and hang up.

"Damn… how am I gonna get out of this shit?" Raven pondered to herself after hanging up the phone and then drifting off to sleep.

Exactly nine hours later, Raven was finally holding her baby and staring at her cell phone that was next to her on the bed while wondering why Kentay hadn't called or texted her back when Jason walked in. In his hands were balloons, two teddy bears, and different types of chocolates. He placed the items on the rolling cart that was beside the bed, washed his hands, and then grabbed the baby from Raven. No words were spoken between the two of them for about five whole minutes. Jason was in love with the baby.

"She sure is big to be six weeks early," Jason said while laying her down in the rolling bassinet.

"This little cutie was right on time," the nurse said in reference to Jason's comment when she walked in. Raven looked like she wanted to disappear. When the nurse saw Raven's face, she just shook her head and turned around and walked back out. She quickly realized that Raven was up to no good, and she had already said too much.

"You lied Raven?" Jason sternly asked.

"No Jason. That was my first time ever seeing that particular nurse. You see she walked right back out so she must have had the wrong room," Raven frantically replied.

Jason stared at her like he was trying to burn a hole through her. They had been having problems in their relationship, but Jason couldn't understand why because he did everything under the sun for Raven. She didn't have to work or pay bills, and she barely cooked and cleaned, but Jason still loved her. Looking at Raven with distrust, he reflected on how they got to this point.

A year and a half ago, Jason had met Raven during one of the lowest points in his life. He was sitting at the bar in the Dark Horse Tavern that was located behind the cheap Budget Inn on highway 182 East drinking his life away, when Raven sat down next to him and rubbed her body up against his while taking his seat. Jason looked up at her and wondered was she even old enough to be in the bar, but he ignored her and ordered his third double shot of Hennessy without ice and downed it without even cringing. Jason had just found out that woman he had proposed to and was planning on marrying had been sleeping with his best man. To add insult to injury, she told him that the baby she was carrying couldn't possibly be his.

To say that he was crushed would be an understatement. The fact that she left a video of her confession along with a sex tape of her and his best friend was what hurt the most. He knew that if he would have been face to face with them, someone would have died, but he was pissed that he didn't have the opportunity because he hadn't seen or heard from either one of them since then. Raven began making small talk with him and one thing led to another. She admitted that she was underage, but had a friend who worked in the bar and let her chill there from time to time. Raven was a little young for Jason's liking, but he was vulnerable at the moment and what was supposed to be a one night fling turned into a full relationship. Jason figured that since Raven was young, he could mold her into the woman she needed to be, but it had been an uphill battle for him. She accused him of robbing her of her innocence, but all he wanted to do was provide for her and make sure that she wanted for nothing.

"Hello. I'm here for you guys to sign the birth certificate," a lady said when she walked in, breaking Jason from his thoughts.

"Can we do that later?" Raven spoke up.

"Why the hell would we have to do it later? If you do to me what she did, there's going to be hell for you to pay," Jason said to Raven without blinking.

Chapter Eighteen

It was the second Monday in October, which was Fall Break for Ole Miss Students. Kya wished that she was at home, but instead, she was stuck in Oxford studying. Blow had managed to turn her life upside down in a matter of months, and she couldn't get rid of him no matter how hard she tried. She had been so caught up with his bullshit that she was on the verge on failing a couple of classes. Most people were gone home for the school holiday, but Kya knew that she needed to get herself together ASAP. She was also trying to figure out a way to get rid of Blow, permanently. Several thoughts entered her mind, but she wasn't sure if she was able to actually go through with any of them.

The ringing of Kya's phone broke her concentration. She glanced at it and saw that it was Ashanti calling, but couldn't bring herself to answer it. Ashanti had actually called Kya quite a few times, but Kya never answered because she didn't want to admit to the things that she had been going through. In Kya's eyes, Ashanti had it made and her life was perfect. She felt like if she admitted to letting a man beat, belittle, and blackmail her, Ashanti would look down on her. After the phone stopped ringing, a text message came through from Shanti that Kya ignored too.

"I gotta get my life together and then we can catch up," Kya said to herself before directing her attention back to her books.

After studying for six straight hours and submitting assignments that her professors allowed her to make up, Kya decided that she could take a little break. Going out should have been the last thing on her mind, but Kya found herself standing in her closet looking for something to throw on, so that she could go to one of the parties on the square. It wasn't a dressy type party, so Kya threw on a white crop top shirt, and some light blue ripped jeans after she got out of the shower. She put her hair up in a messy bun, grabbed her cross over purse, keys, phone, and headed out. The first stop she made was to Wendy's because she was starving. The drive thru line was long as hell, so Kya parked and went inside. After ordering a

Spicy Chicken sandwich meal with a strawberry lemonade, she headed back out of the door and was shocked as hell when she bumped into a familiar face.

"What you doing up this way?" Kya asked. She couldn't understand why she felt so nervous. Maybe it was because of the last conversation she had with Raven, which made her wonder if she had the baby yet or not.

"Had to run up here and handle some business then got hungry as fuck so I stopped by here to grab me a double stack. That drive thru line long as hell," Kentay replied.

"Yep! That's why I went inside," Kya replied while constantly shifting her weight from one foot to the other.

"Why you so nervous? You got a man watching you or some shit?" Tay asked her.

As soon as the words left Kentay's mouth, Kya saw Blow's truck turning into the parking lot on two wheels.

"Oh shit... I gotta go Tay," Kya said and attempted to walk off, but Tay grabbed her by the arm.

"What's wrong?" he asked her.

"What the fuck you doing with your hands on my woman?" Blow stormed up and asked while staring Kentay in the eyes and then looking down at his hand that was still around Kya's arms.

"Blow... this is..." Kya started saying but was cut off.

"Shut the hell up Kya. I didn't ask you shit. I'm talking to this clown ass nigga right here," Blow stated with air in his chest.

"Who the fuck you think you talkin' to you dusty ass muthafucka?" Tay fumed and stepped towards Blow, finally releasing the grip he had on Kya's arm.

"I'm talking to yo ass... now why the fuck you grabbing on my woman?" Blow inquired, not backing down.

Both Blow and Kentay didn't have a fuck to give at the moment. When Tay saw Blow ball his fist and made a move towards him, he quickly moved Kya out of the way, who was standing there trying to intervene, and hit Blow with a quick right, left combo and sent him stumbling backwards. Blood squirted from his nose instantly and Kya screamed because that was the only thing she could do. Once Blow regained his composure, he started making a move towards Tay again, but Kya stood in front of him and began screaming.

"NOOOO!'

"Oh you taking up for this clown?" Blow asked as he stopped his progression and grabbed Kya around the neck instead. She knew from experience that she had fucked up.

Tears started rolling down her face and she just prayed that Blow wouldn't hit her in public. When he released the grasp he had on her neck, she silently thanked God. Noticing the cop turning into the parking lot, Kya knew that was what had just saved her ass. Kentay had quietly gone on inside. Blow headed back to his car but not before kissing Kya so that cop could see and telling her to go to his spot as soon as she left. After making her way to the car and getting in, Kya noticed that she had dropped her food during the scuffle. Her appetite was now gone, so she didn't bother with going back to get it or ordering anything else. She dreadfully put her car in reverse and mentally prepared herself for what was about to go down once she made it to Blow's house.

By the time classes started back the following week, Kya's face still wasn't back to normal from the beating that Blow had put on her. She hid as many of the bruises as she could with makeup, but still ended up wearing sunglasses even though there was no sun in sight. Kya thought she had got away from Amanda before leaving for class, but Amanda noticed all of the makeup right away and confronted her. All of the fussing that Amanda did confirmed to Kya that she made the right decision by not telling Ashanti what was going. She texted Kentay the night of the incident and told him not to mention anything to Shanti. He agreed and told her that if she needed him to take care of that fool to let him know. Kya knew that

Tay didn't like to be disrespected in any type of way and figured that was the reasoning behind his comment.

When Kya's Economics class was over, she gathered her things and headed for the door until she heard her professor calling her name.

"Miss Taylor, could you hold on and speak with me for a minute," Kya heard Dr. McClendon call out to her.

"Shit," Kya cursed under her breath, but she slowed her pace and fell back until the room was clear.

"Miss Taylor… you're a very smart young lady and I can tell that you have a bright future ahead of you, but I can't help but to notice the patterns of your actions as well as some of other disturbing things," Dr. McClendon, a petite black teacher said to Kya. By the time Dr. McClendon was finished talking, Kya already had tears streaming down her face. The professor standing before her was one who let her made up work that she missed. The professor took it a step further by also talking to other teachers on her behalf, so Kya knew that she meant well and couldn't get smart and tell the woman to mind her business no matter how hard she may have wanted to. Kya couldn't bring herself to admit to the things that she was dealing with, but she promised Dr. McClendon that she was going to get it together very soon. When she left campus, the only thing that was on her mid was getting rid of Blow once and for all.

Chapter Nineteen

Ashanti was sitting at a table in Bulldog Deli eating a Spud Max when a familiar girl walked in. After she placed her order, Ashanti noticed that it was a girl that was in her Algebra I class. When she walked by, Shanti motioned for her to join her since she had just got her food and had only taken one bite.

"Ashanti right?" the girl said when she sat down.

"Yep... how do you know my name?" Shanti inquired.

"Who doesn't know your name? You answer all of the questions in class, plus you're Ahmad Jones' girl," the girl simply stated.

Ashanti blushed before responding. "We are just great friends. What's your name though?" Shanti asked her.

"My name is Aaliyah, but everyone calls me Liyah for short," Aaliyah replied and Ashanti choked on her Coke.

"Are you okay?" Liyah asked becoming concerned.

"Yeah, I'm fine. There's just a funny story behind your name. If we hang out in the future, I'll be sure to fill you in," Ashanti old her while chuckling a little.

The girls sat there for about an hour and a half talking about everything under the sun until it was time for Ashanti to head to work for the evening. Even though Ashanti didn't tell her too much of her personal life, she did go ahead and tell her about her and Ahmad's friendship and how she had his number saved in her phone under Aaliyah. Aaliyah laughed with her and told her that she had to think of a new name for him and save hers because she definitely wanted to hang out again. Aaliyah worked at the Bulldog Calling Center, which was right down the street from Bulldog Deli where students called parents and alumni of Mississippi State University soliciting donations for the school. Aaliyah told Ashanti that her biggest pledge to date was for one hundred thousand dollars that came from a season ticket holder who was a member of the alumni association.

When they walked outside, Ahmad was pulling up.

"There goes your 'friend' right there," Aaliyah grinned, being sure to add much emphasis to the word friend. Ashanti laughed at her and walked over to Ahmad's truck.

"When you asked where I was, I didn't know you was coming by here," she said after he opened the door and stepped out.

"You didn't have to know," he replied and pulled her in for a bear hug. Her belly was getting big, but she was still in good shape and beautiful as ever.

"You almost missed me while you tryna do pop ups," Shanti said while giggling.

"I woulda found that ass. I'm headed on campus to practice so I had to stop by here and see my good luck charm," Ahmad said while smiling.

"When is your next home game? I know the next one on the schedule is away," Ashanti stated.

"You keeping up wit me huh? The next home game is next Thursday, and you know I need you there. I want you at the one day after tomorrow, but since it's in Tennessee, I'll let you slide," Ahmad told her.

"I'll definitely be at the one next week," Ashanti told him.

They talked for a few more minutes and went their separate ways. Ashanti wanted to kiss him as bad as he had told her that he wanted to kiss her, but she knew that would only complicate things that much more. She was trying her best to go about things the right way, but the more they saw each other, the harder it became.

"Damn... if only I had met him a few years ago," Ashanti said to herself as she put her truck in gear and headed towards Sports Center.

As soon as Ashanti pulled up at work, her iPhone chimed with a text message. She glanced down and realized that it was Raven's number and immediately became angry.

"Why does this bitch keep fucking with me?" Ashanti said to herself. Raven had texted her a few times before, but Ashanti never opened the messages. She wanted to delete them, but something wouldn't let her. Things had been going great with her and Kentay since the day after the incident, and she feared a message from Raven would only make things worse. When Tay tried to tell her whatever it was that was on his mind, Ashanti told him not to worry about it at the moment because she didn't want to spoil the mood.

When another text message came through, Ashanti finally said fuck it and opened the messages and read all of the texts from the bottom to the top instead of scrolling up first and reading in order.

Raven: Bitch you can keep ignoring me all you want, but I ain't goin nowhere.

Raven: What kinda woman keeps a man from seeing his child?

Raven: Since Tay ain't responding to me, tell him Kendra needs some Dreft washing powder so her skin won't break out.

Raven: We gon be a family whether you like it or not!

Raven: FYI: Tay wasn't running the streets last night, he was at the hospital watching the delivery of his baby.

Raven then sent a picture of the baby.

Raven: Meet Kendra... Kentay's twin!!

Ashanti couldn't move after reading the messages over and over and over. Everything was coming together the more she read.

117

Shanti realized that the night she was robbed at gunpoint, the same night that Tay wanted to go to the basketball game but then changed his mind at the last minute, which happened to be the same night that Raven had the baby. She thought back to how Kentay made love to her and then fixed her breakfast in bed and wanted to tell her something later that day, but she stopped him. Before Ashanti knew what was going on, she had left the parking lot of Sport's Center and was on highway 12 headed towards The Links.

She parked right beside Raven's 1996 Toyota Corolla and got out of her truck without even turning off the ignition. Marching straight to Raven's door, Ashanti beat on it until it was opened. The smirk that Raven had on her face only pissed Ashanti off that much more. It had been two weeks since the incident and all Ashanti could think about was what if she had died that night while Kentay was with her hoe ass ex friend. When Raven opened her mouth to talk, Ashanti stepped forward and punched her directly in it, knocking one of her front teeth down her throat.

Raven screamed out in agony, but it only hyped Ashanti up. She didn't care that she was pregnant. She only cared about beating the fuck out of Raven because in her mind, it was long overdue. Ashanti punched Raven repeatedly in the face and didn't let up until Raven had a tight grip on her Brazilian hair. When Ashanti reached her hands up to grab her hair, Raven found a little strength and kneed Ashanti in the stomach. Luckily for Shanti, she had shifted her weight just in time so the kick wasn't as painful as it could have been. Ashanti stood up and started kicking Raven everywhere that she could.

A few moments later, a baby crying started to drown out Raven's moans and whimpers.

"What the hell is going on?" someone yelled and grabbed Ashanti, which caused her to finally stop kicking Raven. "Ashanti... what are you doing? Oh my God, are you okay?" Jason said after letting go of Ashanti and bending down to check on Raven. "Why are you two fighting? I gotta call an ambulance," Jason said while reaching into his pocket for his phone.

"No… no… I'm… I'm okay," Raven stuttered with her eyes barely open and blood coming out of her mouth.

"Ashanti, why are you fighting your friend after she just had a baby and you're pregnant? What's wrong with y'all?" Jason asked with a voice full of concern.

Ashanti stood there breathing hard and ready to beat Raven some more until a sharp pain pierced through her stomach that caused her to double over in pain. When the baby's cries got louder, Jason hopped up and ran to the back room to check on her. Ashanti's pains subsided for the moment, and she made her way over to Raven and looked down on her with pure disgust.

"I loved you just like you were the sister I never had, but that wasn't enough for you. When you came into my life, everybody told me to stay away from you because you were no good, but I told them no, she's just misunderstood. I gave you the benefit of the doubt. I guess I suck at picking friends because you sure as hell made a fool out of me. Threw you the baby shower of the fucking century only to be humiliated in front of everybody and even on Facebook. You have a great man but that still wasn't enough to satisfy your old dusty, thirsty ass. Nawl, you just had to have mine too. If that baby is Kentay's like you say she is, please believe that he still won't be with your trifling ass. But for now, both of y'all can go to hell and kiss all of my entire ass," Ashanti yelled and kicked Raven one more time before leaving. She heard Jason saying "What the fuck" and calling for her to stop, but Ashanti made her way to her already running truck, hopped in and left.

Ashanti realized that she was supposed to be at work, but she never called in. Not feeling like being bothered or going in at all, she sent her manager a text and told him that she was sick. It wasn't really a lie, because she began to feel terrible. Raven's number started blowing up her phone, but Ashanti ignored the calls. She figured that it was Jason calling because the way Raven was looking when she left, she figured a phone would be the least of her worries. When another pain hit Ashanti, instead of going home, she made a detour and headed for the hospital. Everything started to fade within moments and all Ashanti saw was black.

Chapter Twenty

When Ashanti left, Jason was standing there holding Kendra in shock. Luckily, she had fallen asleep instantly in his arms, so he went and laid her back down in the bassinet. Making slow and cautious steps, he walked over to Raven and stared down at her. The fear was evident in her body language because she began to shake. If her eyes weren't swollen shut, you would probably be able to see fear there too. After what seemed like an eternity, Jason finally spoke.

"So is everything that Ashanti said true?" he softly asked while gauging for her reaction. Even though he had heard every word as clear as day, he hoped that there was some type of logical explanation. "Please tell me what she just said is just some type of misunderstanding, Raven," Jason pleaded in a trembling voice.

"I… I can explain," Raven stuttered barely above a whisper. Before she could say anything else, she started moaning and screaming from pains that were shooting through her body. Jason grabbed Raven's phone and called Ashanti a few times, but she never answered the calls. He was ready to ignore Raven and let her lay there and suffer until he saw blood seeping from under her and onto the floor. It was then that Jason started to panic a little bit. Calling 911, he told them there was emergency and gave the operator details and the address. Raven seemed to be floating in and out of consciousness. He felt for a pulse, and it was weak. The dispatcher assured him that help would be there soon and advised him to stay on the phone until they arrived.

Fifteen minutes later, there was a knock at the door and when Jason opened it, the EMT's rushed in. They began working on Raven right away, checking her pulse, blood pressure, temperature, and everything else while Jason watched in shock. He felt bad for the thoughts he previously had about leaving her there to suffer once they lifted her body and put it on the stretcher, screaming that they had to get her to the hospital right away. They asked Jason questions back to back to back. It wasn't until they asked him if him and

Raven have any prior domestic disputes that he realized he was a suspect.

"We've had problems just like any other couple, and we just had a baby that might not be mine, but I didn't do this," Jason hurriedly stated. As soon as those words left his mouth, he could tell that they came out wrong by the looks on the EMT's faces.

"We're only here to help her, but we are still obligated to report our suspicions. Will you be coming to the hospital sir?" the lady EMT asked.

"The baby is sleeping, but yeah, I will be there as soon as I get her together," Jason responded. He was conflicted about everything that was going on, but he didn't want to cause any trouble for himself by acting like he didn't care.

"I'm sure the cops will be needing more information from you," the lady said and left out of the door. Jason stood there looking dumbfounded for about five minutes before he finally went and prepared Kendra's bag, snuggled her up, and headed out to OCH. Before he left, he quickly grabbed her bag, his phone as well as Raven's, and his car keys. He knew that Raven and her mom didn't see eye to eye, but he still decided to give her a call and let her know what was going on. Before walking out of the door, Jason wondered if he should tell them that Ashanti was responsible or what.

***

Thirty minutes later, Jason and the baby were still sitting in his idle car in the parking lot with the car running to provide them some heat. They had made it to the hospital and found a parking space fifteen minutes after he had left home. However, the weight of everything that had gone down was weighing heavy on his shoulders as he tried to process and make sense of things. When he made it to the hospital, instead of getting right out, Jason pulled out Raven's phone again and clicked on the text message icon. After reading the texts that she had sent Ashanti that day, his blood began to boil. Jason knew that Ashanti had to be telling the truth. He searched for Kentay's name in the text messages, but he didn't find it.

Immediately, he started blaming Kentay for what happened, and an idea popped into his head.

As soon as he made his way inside and asked about Raven, he was directed to a room where two police officers were waiting on him. Before he even had the chance to sit down, they were firing questions at him left and right with notepads in their hands. The only question he answered was the last one, "Did you do this to Raven?"

"No. It was that guy known in the streets as Tay. His real name is Kentay Mills," Jason replied while shaking his head. The name alone caused both officers to perk up, and Jason could tell that he was in the clear as well as Ashanti by the expressions on their faces. He ran down a brief story to them about what happened and added a little to it. Jason knew that Raven more than likely wouldn't uphold his story, so he painted the picture to the cops that she feared he would kill her if she turned him in. That was all they needed to hear. Jason had no idea just how bad the cops wanted to throw the book at Kentay. They had some other irons in the fire at the very moment, but they had to be careful.

"Thanks so much for your time sir. We will have someone come and get you as soon as possible and escort you to see Raven," one of the officers said while shaking Jason's hand and exiting the room.

"The pleasure was all mine," Jason replied while smiling.

Jason smiled down at Kendra, and it hit him for the first time that Raven had given her a name that started with K, which was probably after Kentay.

"You're my baby girl no matter what. Your mommy will pay for what she's done, but you're still my daughter," Jason told Kendra sweetly.

Chapter Twenty-One

"Thank God you're finally awake," Tina said after her daughter began to stir. "What happened Ashanti? You barely made it to the hospital. Thank God you did!" her mom continued rambling.

"What are you doing here mom?" Ashanti asked, puzzled by her mother's presence.

"Well, you sent me a text in a group with the word 'hospital'.I suppose the other number belongs to this fine young man here," Tina blushingly replied.

Ashanti looked to the right where her mom was pointing and saw Ahmad standing there with a worried expression all over his face.

"Are you okay? What happened?" he finally asked.

Ashanti actually remembered everything that happened except texting them. She wasn't ashamed of what she had done because if she had the chance, she would do it all over again. But, telling the story to her mom and Ahmad at the same time was had her feeling some type of way. After a few moments of silence, Ashanti finally told them everything that had transpired right after she left Bulldog Deli and headed to work.

"So this Jason fella put his hands on you?" Ahmad inquired after she was done with her story.

"Not in a bad way," Ashanti answered. "How's my baby?" Shanti finally asked with a voice full of panic while rubbing her stomach. The looks on both Mrs. McNeal and Ahmad's faces caused Ashanti's heart to start beating faster. "Oh my God! What's wrong?" Shanti asked as tears welled up in her eyes.

"Sweetheart, you're actually in labor now, but they are trying to stop it. We didn't know what all happened before you got here, but from what the doctors are saying, it's just one of those things that can't be explained," Tina told her daughter with tears in her own eyes.

"This is all my fault... if I deliver now. What exactly does that mean?" Ashanti asked in a voice full of concern and worry. She could see that there was something her mom wasn't telling her.

"There are some concerns, but the doctor didn't confirm anything, so for now we won't even talk about it," Tina said remotely.

"Mom, I have the right to know what's going on," Ashanti retorted.

"Everything is gon' be alright. You just relax," Ahmad told Ashanti while caressing her right hand.

By now, the tears that Ashanti had been fighting back were flowing freely down her face. Ahmad grabbed some Kleenex from by the sink and wiped her tears away. Ashanti was thankful to have him by her side, but she couldn't help but to wonder where Kentay was.

"You know I don't care much for that whatever he is of yours, but where is he?" Mrs. McNeal asked, as if she was reading her daughter's mind.

"I was just about to ask that, but..." Ashanti said and cut her words off when she locked eyes with Ahmad.

"It's cool. I understand. He needs to be here, but I'll be here until I know he's on the way," Ahmad stated emphatically.

Ashanti asked for her phone and her mom handed it to her and told her that she must have dropped it after she passed out while trying to get out of her truck. Ashanti didn't remember that either so she didn't reply. She noticed she had some text messages, but ignored them for the moment and called Kentay. His phone went straight to voicemail, so Shanti tried again. After getting the same results three times in a row, Ashanti sent him a text message saying that something was wrong and she needed him.

125

"Let me guess, the no good nigga didn't answer," Tina said with disgust etched in her voice. Ashanti didn't bother replying. She just clicked on her other messages and noticed that she really did text her mom and Ahmad in a group. Ashanti clicked on a message from the real Aaliyah and told her what was going on.

Out of nowhere, pains started erupting through Ashanti's abdomen back to back to back causing her to scream and grasp uncontrollably. Ahmad hit the nurse's button right away while Tina tried her best to comfort her daughter. Monitors started beeping, and within seconds, the room was filled with nurses and doctors. Ahmad and Tina were asked to leave, but they didn't move a step until they forced to do so. One of the nurses gently nudged them and told them if they wanted the best care possible for the patient, then they should exit and allow the staff to do their job. Ashanti was in so much pain, she had no idea what was going on. She heard someone saying something about hitting a button for pain and something about an epidural, but within minutes, she was out like a light.

***

Pacing the floor in the waiting room, both Ahmad and Mrs. McNeal were silent for about five whole minutes. Tina couldn't bring herself to tell her daughter everything the doctor had said, so instead, she silently prayed for a miracle. It was hurting her to see her daughter go through what she was dealing with. The doctor had previously told them that the sac had busted, and the umbilical cord was wrapped around the baby's neck. While Ashanti was sedated, they had been trying everything possible to reverse the situation, but it was looking impossible to them. It was stated that if Ashanti had been feeling any moves and kicks, then they were probably faint. After further examination and many tests ran, it appeared that she had a slow leaking amniotic sac and by speculation, that was when the cord moved. It happens a lot andmost women mistake it for urine or discharge.

About fifteen minutes later, a girl walked up and spoke to Ahmad. Tina looked at her like she was crazy, and she introduced herself right away.

"I'm Aaliyah, Ashanti's friend. She texted me and told me what was going on so I came right over," Aaliyah told them.

"Oh you're Aaliyah. Ashanti has mentioned you," Ahmad stated after recognizing the name.

"Well, you know she talks about you, but don't tell her I said it," Liyah stated, trying to make light of the entire situation because everyone seemed to be a nervous wreck judging by the expressions on their faces. They all finally sat down and made small talk while waiting to hear from the doctor.

***

"You're gonna feel a lot of pressure, but just push when we say push," the doctor told Ashanti.

"Arrggghhhhh!!!" Ashanti screamed out as another contraction hit her.

"Are you sure we can't give her an epidural? She's having to deal with enough," one of the nurses said.

"It's too risky considering the circumstances," Dr. Brown replied.

The nurse seemed to be feeling really sorry for Ashanti because she squeezed her hands and gave her a smile. Ashanti tried her best to return the smile, but another pain hit her and all she could do was yell.

"One more big push Ashanti," Dr. Brown coaxed her.

Ashanti pushed as hard as she could and a few moments later, she saw the doctor pulling her baby out of her.

"Oh my God... what's wrong? Isn't he supposed to be crying?" Ashanti said in a panic. As soon as the words left her mouth, she saw Dr. Brown hit the baby on his bottom, but he still didn't cry. "NOOOOO NOOOO NOOOO!!! WHAT'S WRONG WITH MY BABY??" Ashanti screamed hysterically.

"Give her a dose of Oxycodone ASAP," Dr. Brown ordered.

The nurse complied right away and Ashanti's cries faded away as she drifted off into a deep sleep within minutes.

***

Dr. Brown headed to the waiting room where Ashanti's family was waiting, so that he could break the news to them. Once he made it, he noticed that they weren't alone, so he called them out and escorted them to a private room. Once they were all gathered, Tina, Ahmad, and Aaliyah, he began talking.

"It is with great sympathy and regret that I inform you of your loss. Ashanti is heavily sedated, as she will be for the next couple of days, but the baby didn't make it. He was stillborn, so there was never a chance of survival. She is going to be an emotional wreck, and she will need all of the support that she can get. You guys are welcome to see the baby after we get him cleaned up, and it will be up to her on what type of arrangements she wants. He was born weighing four pounds and three ounces. Once again, I'm sorry and if there is anything I can do, please don't hesitate to let me know," Dr. Brown said and hugged each of them before exiting the room. After he left and they were all alone, Tina broke down and Ahmad as well as Aaliyah comforted her as best as they could while shedding tears of their own.

Chapter Twenty-Two

"Man we haven't dipped like this in a minute, and honestly with everything that's going on, I can't believe you left town. I mean I know we got eyes and ears in the streets, but it ain't nothing like us being there to handle shit ourselves," Slick said to his boy.

"Man I swear to you, if I didn't dip out… an innocent muthafucka was bout to catch a bullet. Raven been blowing my shit up so got damn much, I just cut it off. Ima have to call my baby in a few though," Kentay replied.

"So you really think that baby yours dawg?" Slick inquired.

"I believe so… I know I done fucked up for real for real now," Tay said while shaking his head.

"You gon' get a blood test though right?" Slick earnestly asked.

"Yeah. If I just claim the baby without getting a test you know Shanti gon be pissed the fuck off. I haven't even told her yet. I started to one day, but shit been going so good, she didn't even wanna hear it," Tay retorted.

"I feel ya, but you better tell her before Raven does. That shit would really set her off. Shanti a good girl, but you know she don't like being disrespected and Raven a foul bitch," Slick conveyed his opinion.

They had hopped on the jet the night before and were now chilling out on the beach in Puerto Rico smoking a blunt. The business side of the trip had been handled earlier that morning, and the rest would be pleasure until they left the next morning. Kentay decided to take the trip himself and stay out of dodge ,so that whoever was brave enough to break in his shit would slip up again. He wasn't tripping too much because he knew it was only a matter of time before he got his revenge.

"You better go on and call your girl because you know she gon' be worried. And you said shit been going good, so don't fuck it up," Slick told Tay.

"Yeah you right. I'm bout to, right after these two hoes that's walking up break us off wit some head," Tay replied while smirking.

The chocolate girl with the long blonde weave must have heard what Kentay said, because she walked straight up to him and grabbed his dick.

"You better be glad ya dick big or I was bout to clown yo ass. Now come on let me suck you off," the girl told him.

"Just like I like em, bold as hell. Ya skills better be superb or Ima clown yo ass," Tay said while laughing and following her.

Slick didn't talk shit like Tay did, but it turned out that he didn't have to at that moment. The other girl removed his dick from his shorts and covered it with her mouth as soon as she made it close to him. No words were ever spoken. When she finished, he reached in his pocket and broke her off with two or three hundred dollars; he didn't count it. In his eyes, it was worth it because she swallowed every drop of his cum.

Twenty minutes later, Tay walked back with a smile big as fuck on his face.

"You fucked her too didn't you? I hope yo ass strapped up nigga," Slick said while laughing.

"Yep and hell yeah my nigga, I ain't getting caught up no mo," Tay clarified. "Let me call my baby now," he continued.

As soon as he powered his phone on, text messages started coming through. Ignoring all of the ones from Raven and a few other hoes, Kentay clicked on Shanti's name and hopped up after he read her message.

Shanti: *Something is wrong. I need you and I'm at the hospital!!!*

"What's wrong bruh?" Slick asked after he hopped up himself.

"Shanti man… she said something wrong, and she at the hospital. She need me. I gotta get outta here," Tay said and headed back to his suite. He had just made plans to hook up with the girl he had just met later on that night, but that shit was dead now.

"I'm calling the pilot now," Slick called behind him and did just what he said.

"Damn if something happen I don't know what Ima do. I shouldn't have left," Tay fumed.

"Think positive man. We can leave in three hours and will get there bout five in the morning," Slick relayed the message to Kentay he had just received.

"Fuck! Then I'll still have like two and a half hours to drive to Starkville. This is some fucking bullshit," Tay practically yelled.

"I'm bout to call him back, but that's probably the best he can do. And it beats getting there tomorrow evening," Slick said in an attempt to try and calm his boy down.

The two of them went to their separate suites, packed their bags, and met back up in the lobby of the hotel an hour later. Within another hour and a half, they were up in the air headed back home with thoughts consuming their minds so much that they didn't even talk. Both of them downed two double shots of Crown Vanilla as soon as they were seated, but it didn't do much to calm their nerves.

"I just gotta get to her and my baby," Kentay finally said, breaking the deadening silence.

"Won't be long man. It won't be much longer," Slick told his boy. They both drifted off to sleep and were awakened by the roughness when they landed. Kentay checked the time and saw that the pilot had cut an hour off the flight because it was four o'clock. He didn't talk to Ashanti's mom too much, but he did have her number. So, he sent her a text telling her that he had been out of town on business, but he would be at the hospital no later than seven o'clock. He had every intention of keeping his word and being there before then. After gassing up, Kentay hopped on highway 25 and headed north and didn't plan on stopping anymore until he made it to Starkville.

At 6:23 am, Kentay was backing into a parking space at Oktibbeha County Hospital. He called Mrs. McNeal to find out exactly where they were and she told him. On his way in, he saw the basketball player Ahmad Jones once again and wanted to talk to him about something, but he knew now wasn't the time because he heard a lot of pain in Tina's voice.

"I'll catch up with him sooner or later," Tay said as he hopped on the elevator. He had a bad feeling in the pit of his stomach that wasn't there before arriving at the hospital. Inwardly, Kentay wished that he had smoked a blunt before walking inside. He knew that Slick would pulling up soon because he had dropped him off at his ride that wasn't too far away.

Kentay got off of the elevator and looked at the signs that pointed to the room numbers and headed right after he saw the one that he was looking for. Before he made it to the room, Mrs. Tina and another girl who Kentay didn't know walked out.

"She woke up screaming about having a nightmare so they gave her more meds and put her back to sleep," Tina told Kentay and led him towards the waiting area that they had become all too familiar with.

"What's wrong? What happened?" Kentay asked once they were all alone. Tina got choked up and couldn't find the words to say, so Aaliyah took over.

"I'm Aaliyah, Ashanti's friend," she introduced herself first.

"Aaliyah… I've heard about how close y'all are. Nice to finally meet you," Kentay replied.

"Likewise. Well… there's no easy way to say any of this, but Ashanti was having a few complications that she knew nothing about. Then, she was in a fight with Raven, and as a result to everything, she went into labor," Aaliyah slowly stated.

"What the fuck? Is she okay? Is my baby okay?" Kentay asked but when Tina broke down, he knew something was terribly wrong.

"Ashanti will be fine in time. She really thinks that she had a bad dream, so they are keeping her sedated, but... the baby... he didn't make it," Aaliyah said as she finally failed at fighting back her own tears.

Kentay lost it. He punched the wall several times, leaving holes and blood from his fingers on it.

"What the fuck? No! I don't believe this shit. I gotta see her. I gotta see my baby," Kentay fumed and headed towards Ashanti's room.

"Please don't wake her up Kentay," Tina called out to him but he kept going, leaving the two of them in the waiting area. When he walked into Shanti's room and looked at her, he broke down in tears.

"I'm so sorry baby. I promise Ima make this up to you," Kentay sobbed. Ashanti's once big round belly was gone. She still looked pregnant, but her stomach wasn't as big as it was the last time Kentay saw her. Instead of looking seven months pregnant, she now looked how she did at four months to him.

Kentay started punching the walls in the room, and two nurses ran in and asked him to leave. He didn't want to leave Ashanti, but his emotions were getting the best of him. Plus, he knew that he had to be cooperative to keep them from calling security.

"I wanna see my baby," Kentay said after he was outside of the door.

"Are you sure?" one of the nurses asked him.

The look he gave her stopped either of them from asking any more questions.

"Follow me... and since she's so sedated, you'll have to decide what you want to do with the body. He weighed a little over five pounds at birth," the nurse told him. Kentay followed closely behind, not knowing what to say or do. They bypassed the waiting room. He saw Slick standing there talking to Tina and Aaliyah, but he kept following the nurses. He could tell by the look on Slick's face that they had broken the news to him.

When they made it down to the basement, the coldness was no match for what Kentay felt in his heart. The nurses led the way over the smallest body in the room. He stared down at the body of his lifeless son and broke down uncontrollable again. The nurses comforted him as best as they could. They told him to try and make a decision before the day was over with on what to do with the body. He advised them to call West Funeral Home and have them set up a graveside service and spare no expenses. The nurses took notes and told him that they would take care of everything. Even though Ashanti was only seven months pregnant, the baby was five pounds, and Kentay could tell that he was the splitting image of him. It scared him when he looked down. By the time he was done with his visit, his sorrow and pity had turned to anger and only one thing was on his mind. Revenge.

Chapter Twenty-Three

"Girl, you have been moping around for far too long. When I first met you a few months ago, you were so vibrant and full of life. You gotta get it together," Amanda said.

"I wish I could rewind and never met some people that I met a few months ago. My life has been a living hell since I met Blow, but I'm back on track with school and that's all that matters right now," Kya depressingly said.

"But you were balancing both in the beginning. Get rid of Blow's ass. It can't be that hard," Amanda stated, trying to empathize with her roommate.

"I wish it was that simple. I'm thinking about transferring next semester. Since I took the majority of my core classes, I might go on to UMC in Jackson. It just depends," Kya told her roommate.

"Don't let Blow run you away. You need to focus and carry on with your original plans," Amanda retorted. "Besides. That sounds stressful as hell," she continued.

"I don't know but I'm thinking hard about it. We'll see," Kya replied. "There are just some things that you don't know. I'm in a fucked up situation and running sounds pretty good right about now," Kya said poignantly.

"Yeah but if you run, you'll be looking over your shoulders for the rest of your life. Who wants to live like that? I don't and I know you ain't even that type. I know we just met each other, but I'm here if you need me for anything." Amanda sincerely stated.

Since they were sitting in their room talking, Kya decided to open up about everything that had been going on in her life. She told Amanda about her summer first and how excited and ready she was to start school. Kya even told her about her friendship with Ashanti and Raven and how they all have drifted apart. She admitted to being at fault because Ashanti had been reaching out to her and said that she would just wait and go visit her over the Thanksgiving holidays. The story about how she met Blow, and the things that he had been doing and had her doing were told last. Kya told her story with her hands on her temples and her eyes closed. When she finally finished talking, she expected Amanda to call her stupid, dumb, crazy, and everything under the sun. To her surprise, when she opened her eyes, she found Amanda in tears. Instead of talking, she simply got up and gave Kya a long and considerate hug.

They embraced and cried in each other's arms for what seemed like forever.

"Come on… we about to go shopping. Retail therapy always does the trick and we can talk more in the car," Amanda said, finally breaking the silence.

"I don't need anything, but I guess the least I can do is spend some of the money Blow breaks me off with. That's the only good thing about him, but I'd rather not have the money and be free. I need to text him though," Kya said.

"Do what you gotta do, but hurry up. I'm glad we both got out of class early today," Amanda said as she threw on some BKE skinny jeans, an Ole Miss tee and her red converse. Kya sent Blow a text and waited for a reply as she put on her red and black Jordan's. She never took her clothes off after class like Amada did, so she already had on an Ole Miss tee similar to Amanda's and some ripped boyfriend ankles jeans.

Kya: Hey babe. Me and Amanda bout to go do a lil shopping. You need anything?

Blow: Nah. Just hit me up when you get back.

Kya: Alright (kissy face)

"Ugh… I still gotta play nice until I figure this shit out," Kya said as they were headed to Amanda's car.

"You're a smart girl. I know you'll figure it out soon," Amanda told her after she hit the alarm to lock the doors. They hopped in and Amanda told Siri to navigate to the Wolfchase Galleria in Memphis. She knew how to get to Germantown Parkway because she frequented the mall often since she was from Cordova, but she just loved hearing the directions out loud.

Kya and Amanda talked the entire ride to the mall, and Amanda helped Kya put a lot of things into perspective. Amanda also shared pieces of her life with Kya to let her know that everyone has issues. It had Kya feeling a whole lot better, and she couldn't help but to be thankful for meeting and connecting with Amanda. She did miss Ashanti deep down and something told her that they would probably never be close as they once were. However, she did vow to go and visit her the next month.

After making it to the mall, the first stop they made was to Victoria Secret. Kya and Amanda both got a couple of PINK joggers and some bra and panty sets that were on sale. Kya always saved most of the money Blow gave her, but she knew she had to have something to show for it most times, so she went to Belk and bought one of the new MK purses. After hitting up Journey's and getting another pair of converse, they headed to the food court. Kya grabbed a Philly Cheesesteak from Steak Escape while Amanda decided to grab some shrimp fried rice, sweet and sour chicken, and sesame chicken from the Chinese restaurant.

On the way back, they talked about which parties they wanted to hit up the weekend and also made plans to visit each other's hometowns in the near future. Kya warned Amanda that she was from deep in the woods and told her not to rush. They laughed it off. Kya couldn't help but to smile and be grateful for the newfound friendship that was developing between her and Amanda. When they made it back to Oxford, Kya's mind went right back to the thoughts that had been consuming it for the past few weeks. Getting rid of Blow's crazy ass. She reluctantly texted him and let him know that she was back. He instantly replied back to her announcement by telling her to come and hop on his big black dick.

"This muthafucka is really delusional," Kya mumbled and shook her head while reading his reply. After taking her bags inside, she grabbed her overnight bag and mentally prepared herself to go and jump on the little shrimp between Blow's legs that he thought was a dick.

Chapter Twenty-Four

Raven was lying in the hospital bed thanking God that the pain medication her doctor had given her finally kicked in. She was in agonizing pain. Her doctor informed her that she was a very lucky woman to endure all of the things that she had gone through in such a short period of time. He strongly recommended that she take it easy from now on because her body had gone through a lot. He was discharging her after being in the hospital for two days. As she thought about going home, the notion was bittersweet to her because she knew that she would have to answer to Jason. He was so upset with her that he hadn't even been back to the hospital. Instead, Jason sent her mom to pick her up knowing how strained their relationship was. As soon as Raven made eye contact with her mom, her mouth began.

"Jason told me about everything you've done. You trifling just like yo no good daddy," Raven's mom huffed.

"Who picked him?" Raven replied and rolled her eyes. Before her mom could respond, the nurse walked through the door with a wheelchair and discharge papers.

"Look what I got for you! I know you're ready to get home and see that precious baby girl of yours," the nurse said to Raven while smiling.

"I sure am," Raven replied while standing up.

"Well let's get you out of here," the nurse said while moving towards the bed to assist Raven.

After a few minute of maneuvering around, they were headed out of the door and towards the elevator. Raven was self-conscious about the way she looked because both of her eyes had black marks around them. In addition, she also had other bruises to her face as well as her entire body. The internal bleeding had stopped and her stitches were sewn back together. Before Jason left the hospital the other day, he explained to her what he told the cops and threatened her to stick with the story. When the cops visited her the day before, all she did was cried, and the hospital administration asked them to leave. They left with the promise that they would be in touch with her real soon.

Once they made it outside, the wind was chilly. Raven's mom went and got the car and drove up to the front of the hospital instead of having the nurse wheel her all the way out. Raven knew she only did that kind gesture because they weren't alone. Across the parking lot, Raven spotted Kentay's truck and tensed up. A small part of her wondered if he was coming to check on her, but the threat that Jason gave her made her want to stay on the straight and narrow for a little while. Kentay appeared to be in one of his moods when he got out of his truck. Raven could tell by the way he was biting his jaws because that was something he did when he was pissed off. She hurriedly got into her mom's car to keep him from seeing her with the intent to call him as soon as Jason left for work again.

The ride to Raven's place was quiet. She didn't offer any words to her mom, and her mom acted like she was riding by herself. When they pulled up to The Links, Raven got out and slammed the door without saying thank you or anything. Her mom drove off while shaking her head. As Raven headed to her apartment, she couldn't help but to shake her head at the relationship of her and her mom and the reasoning behind it.

As soon as Raven got off of the bus and entered the house after school, she went straight to the kitchen and opened the refrigerator. It was her first year of junior high and she always gave her lunch away to the football boys to gain attention from them. On this particular, day, she was super excited because it was the 8th, which meant it was stamp day and she the fridge was about to be lit. To her surprise, she opened the door to their beige refrigerator and the only thing she saw was eggs and butter.

"I know this bitch better not sold the stamps again before buying food," Raven fumed as she stormed towards her mother's room.

When she was close to the room, she heard her mom screaming and moaning. Raven sucked her teeth and was about to head to her room until she heard her mom say the name Kevin.

"I know that ain't Uncle Kevin," Raven said as her curiosity got the best of her. Easing towards the room, Raven noticed that the door was cracked and looked inside. She saw her mom fucking her best friend's husband and from the looks of it, they were very familiar with each other. Raven shook her head and walked towards the living room. After spotting her mom's purse on the end table, she grabbed the wallet and found the EBT card and smiled. "I'm going to the West Side store and get me something to eat since they take these cards." Raven said to herself.

Before Raven could make it out the door, Tisha, her mom's best friend was knocking on the door.

"Hey Auntie Tisha," Raven greeted her.

"Where's your mom?" Tisha asked. Raven automatically looked towards the hall unintentionally. Tisha took that as a sign to head towards her friend's bedroom like she always did when she came to visit. Raven called out to her, but Tisha told her that she would be right back. "What the fuck?" Tisha screamed. Raven didn't even care to go and see what was going on. She was used to her mom doing trifling things, but she never thought that she would sleep with Kevin. Cussing, yelling, screaming, glass being shattered, and a lot of bumping and banging could be heard from the front.

Ten minutes later, Tisha was storming out of the front door pissed the fuck off. Kevin was right behind her apologizing and begging. Before she was all the way out of the door, she turned around to Raven and gave her a death stare before leaving.

"You knew what your hoe ass mama was doing didn't you... I hope you don't grow up to be like her, but neither of y'all better not look my way anymore or I'm gonna send you to meet your maker," Tisha said and left.

"You know you coulda stopped her. You did this shit on purpose. You ain't shit just like your no good daddy," Raven's mom

141

yelled at her and walked up to her and slapped her so hard she saw stars.

"I don't know why she hates me, I'm just like her," Raven admitted to herself before unlocking her apartment door and walking inside.

"Jason! I'm home," Raven called out after she made it inside. She found it strange that the TV nor lights were on but headed to the back towards Kendra's room. Raven's heart dropped, and she gasped loudly after turning on the lights and seeing a completely empty room. She walked all over the apartment calling Jason's name but not getting an answer. When she walked back in the living room, she finally noticed a handwritten note on the table and picked it up and read it.

Kendra is my baby regardless of what a fucking blood test says. You aren't fit to be a mother, and she's better off without you. Spend your time chasing behind no good ass men and screwing your best friend's man you worthless piece of human being like you have been doing. See how that works out for you. You ain't shit! And now, you won't have shit anymore either. Your ass had it made, but you didn't appreciate it. Now, you reap what you fucking sow. Have fun paying your own fucking way. By the way... Don't bother looking for us because you'll never find us!!

Raven was speechless after reading Jason's note about twenty times. When it finally sank in that he had taken her child, all she could think about was how that was the only link between her and Kentay. She screamed senseless over and over until her voice was gone.

Chapter Twenty-Five

"Shanti, baby… you gotta eat something sweetheart," Mrs. Tina said to her daughter.

"I'm really not hungry," Ashanti replied with her eyes closed.

"But you need to Ashanti. They are gonna put that tube in you to feed you if you don't start eating on your own soon. The doctor is thinking about letting you out today or tomorrow if you'll eat. I know you gotta be tired of being in here," Tina pleaded with Shanti. "Do I need to get Ahmad back over here?" she continued.

Ashanti finally opened her eyes and looked at her mom. Ahmad had recently left because he had an out of town basketball game to go to. He offered to skip it, but for the first time, Ashanti spoke up and told him that she wouldn't allow him to do that.

"Fine… I'll eat a little. Only because I don't want you bothering him," Ashanti replied.

"Good because if she didn't call, I was going to grab your phone and call him myself," Aaliyah countered.

"Sweetheart, I know this sounds all cliché, and you probably don't wanna hear it, but God makes no mistakes and we will get through this," Tina said trying her best to comfort her daughter.

"Mom, you're right… that is cliché and I don't wanna hear it, but thanks for trying," Ashanti patronized.

A few minutes later, Ashanti sat up while her mom fed her some of the food on her tray, which consisted of hamburger steak, mashed potatoes, broccoli, and sweet tea. Ashanti ate about half, which was good because she hadn't been eating anything. When the door swung open, everyone assumed it was the doctor. However, it was Kentay who came strolling in holding balloons, candy, and a bear.

Ashanti rolled her eyes at him and laid back down in the bed, making sure that her back was facing him.

"Can y'all give us a minute please," Ashanti heard Kentay saying to her mom and friend.

"Are you okay with that Shanti?" Mrs. McNeal asked before leaving her daughter alone with Kentay.

"Y'all don't have to leave unless y'all want to. Y'all know everything anyway," Ashanti replied. After she made that comment, Tina remained comfortable in her chair, and Aaliyah didn't move either. Kentay looked back and forth between Tina and Aaliyah, pleading with his eyes for them to leave. But, they didn't budge from their spots so finally made his way around to the side of the bed where Ashanti was facing.

"Baby… your mom filled me in on what happened. You know Ima do everything I can to make it right. I know I should've told you when I left and when the baby was born, but everything was going so great with us, and you told me not to. Words can't even describe how sorry I am baby, but I promise you I will make it right, no matter what… I gotta," Kentay stated with tears in his eyes. "I got a graveside ceremony set up. I know you didn't want him to be a junior, so just name him so I can finalize everything," he continued. Ashanti had tears rolling down her face as Kentay talked. "Please don't give up on us Shanti, please baby," he pleaded with her as he wiped her tears away. Ashanti laid there listening to Kentay pour his heart out. Before he arrived, she had envisioned herself cussing him out and telling him to leave. Now after hearing him talk, all she could do was cry. In her mind, she still wanted to tell him that they needed a break, but the words just would not come out. After a few minutes of crying, there was a knock at the door, and the doctor walked in.

"Ms. McNeal… are you ready to get out of here?" he asked her.

Ashanti was so confused that she shook and nodded her head.

"Come on and take a walk with me," he told her. When she made a move to get up, Kentay quickly helped her and then wiped the rest of her tears away. Ashanti slowly made her way over to the doctor. She had been up walking a little the day before, and the doctor mainly did it to keep her from sinking deeper into depression. Physically, she was fine, but her mental state was a different story.

"You ready to go home?" Dr. Brown asked Ashanti as they walked down the hall.

"Yeah, it's gonna be difficult but I'm ready to get out of here," Ashanti disappointingly replied.

"I'm going to let you go today, that way you'll have three days to relax, and then on Monday, I want you to get back into your normal routine. This was an unfortunate situation, but you're very young and I have faith that you'll bounce back. I'm giving you a prescription for pain as well as depression to take as needed. Many people run from anti-depressants, but it's only to help you cope with the traumatic experience you're dealing with," Dr. Brown stated as he empathize with his patient.

"Okay. How soon before I leave?" Ashanti inquired.

"Not very long. The discharge papers are done, they just have to be signed and dated," he told her. They talked for a few more minutes and then headed back to the room.

Ashanti walked back into her room and told everyone that she was being discharged. She found it hard to look Kentay in the face. She knew that he loved her, but asked herself was love really enough.

"I'll go and pull my truck up to the front," Kentay said and started towards the door.

"I'm staying with my mom until Monday," Ashanti said, stopping Kentay in his tracks. She could tell that she caught him off guard by the expression on his face when she finally made eye contact with him.

"I'm gonna take care of you baby," Tay pleaded with her.

"I just need my mom Tay. It's nothing against you," Ashanti lied. She couldn't bring herself to stay at her apartment and to deal with Kentay at the moment.

"Alright Shanti. I don't like it, but I can't do nothing but respect it. I'll drop you off there so Ima still go pull my truck up closer," Tay said before he walked out.

Almost an hour later, Ashanti was being wheeled out of the hospital where Kentay was waiting on her. She gave her mom her prescriptions to go and get filled and told her that she was going to pack a bag and she would be there shortly. Aaliyah hugged her and told her that she had been taking care of all of her assignments and told her not to be surprised if she saw her before Monday. Ashanti thanked her for being so kind and gave her another hug before Kentay helped her get in the truck. They rode in silence as Kentay headed to Carpenter Place. Ashanti closed her eyes and pretended to be asleep to keep from talking on the eight minute drive to her place.

Being the gentleman that he had been all day, Kentay rushed around to open Ashanti's door after he parked and helped her out. Ashanti wished that he was always the gentleman that he was displaying at the moment and not only because he felt guilty. When they made it inside, Ashanti walked towards her bedroom, but stopped at the door of the baby's room. She put her hand on the knob but didn't turn it.

"Don't do this to yourself right now baby," Kentay softly spoke. Tears came out of nowhere and streamed down Ashanti's cheeks. She wanted to open the door, but she knew that her emotions would overwhelm her, so she slowly headed towards her room, grabbed her small suitcase, and started filling it with her clothes and toiletries. It only took her fifteen minutes to pack, and she was ready to go.

"You want me to stay at your mom's house with you?" Kentay asked after they were in the truck and on their way.

"Nah… I'll be good. You just go and do you like you always do," Ashanti replied nonchalantly. Kentay sighed and Ashanti could tell she had struck a nerve when she saw him biting the inside of his jaw, something he always did when he was angry. The rest of the ride was quiet, and she was thankful for it. When they made it to Tina's house, Ashanti saw her Range Rover parked in the yard and figured her mom had brought it there right after she was admitted to the hospital. Kentay took Ashanti's suitcase in and assisted her as well. Her mom was pulling up right when she pulled her key from her purse.

"Please don't make this a permanent thing. I will do anything I can to make this right. I love you!" Kentay told her.

"I love you too, but is love really enough?" Ashanti said and headed towards her room leaving Kentay standing there looking flabbergasted.

Chapter Twenty-Six

When Kentay left Ashanti's mom house, he wanted to turn around and go be with Ashanti, but he didn't know whether that would help or hurt them. Thinking for a few minutes, he decided that it was probably best to give her some space, so he shifted his attention elsewhere. Raven had been blowing him up, but he refused to answer her calls or even read her text messages because the shit she pulled was foul in his eyes, and he wanted to strangle her ass. Tay admitted to himself that he was responsible for the bullshit, but he thought that he had everything under control. His cell phone rang, breaking him from his reverie.

"What up homie?" Kentay answered after the call connected to his Bluetooth.

"Word on the street, some nigga tryna get rid of some bricks. They say he been talking to a few people about it, and I heard from Deon that the same dude been bragging bout copping some shit from some cats in Memphis," Slick told his boy.

"Oh yeah… well that's right up my muthafuckin alley. I hope whoever this pussy ass nigga is, he make a move soon because I'm tired of sitting back waiting. It's been too long," Tay sternly stated.

"I feel ya boss man, but calm down. This shit is really playing out exactly how it's supposed to. We knew a nigga wasn't gon rob one day and flaunt the next day. It's all lining up,' Slick replied.

"Yeah you right. Just so much bullshit going on and somebody bout to catch a beat down behind all this shit," Tay fumed.

"How Shanti doing man? You got everything situated for tomorrow?" Slick inquired.

"I believe she bout done wit my ass, but I ain't letting no other nigga have her. She at her mom's house," Tay said sounding a little defeated.

"You prolly just gotta give her time. This a lot she dealing wit, but you gotta still be there for her even if she push you away. You heard from Raven?" Slick asked.

"Damn… she been blowing me up, and you just talked her up again. Let me check this bitch right quick," Tay told Slick and ended the call before he could respond.

"What the fu…" Kentay started saying until he Raven screamed uncontrollably and cut him off.

"Jason… baby… gone… help…" were the only words Kentay heard Raven say.

"Yo, calm the fuck down and talk because I can't hear shit you sayin," he told her.

"Jason took… took Kendra and I have no idea where he's gone," Raven finally said after calming down and catching her breath.

"The fuck you mean took? What the hell happened Raven? And don't think I don't know about that shit you pulled with Ashanti," Tay heatedly seethe.

"I'm sorry about all that… but I don't know where he went. He's not answering the phone or anything. He's left me a note," Raven said while still crying.

Kentay listened to her read the note and shook his head. He didn't know what the fuck to think or do. Him and Ashanti had just lost their baby ,and now, the baby he had with Raven had been kidnapped.

"Raven, the baby does resemble me, but until we get a blood test, I can't get emotionally attached. Are you sure it's mine anyway?" Kentay inquired.

"Tay you know good and got damn well that's your baby. I know you probably hope it ain't so Ashanti can be the only one with your child, but newsflash… YOU HAVE TWO!!" Raven screamed. After she said that, Kentay realized that she didn't know what happened after the fight. Deep down, he knew the baby was his, but he owed to Ashanti to at least get tested at not make it look like he wanted the baby.

"Fuck!! Ima have to talk to you later. I got too much other shit I'm dealing wit right now, but I'll holla at ya later," Tay said and hung up before Raven could reply. He knew it wouldn't be right to discuss Ashanti's situation with Raven and staying on the phone would have led to just that. When Tay got close to the Dark Horse Tavern, he turned his signal on and made the right turn because he needed a drink to relax his mind and be able to think.

Two hours and six drinks later, Kentay found his self on the way to Raven's apartment. His plans were instantly changed when he noticed blue lights up ahead. It was Friday night so he didn't know whether it was a road block or if the police had someone pulled over. The only thing he did know was that he didn't want to be near the cops at all so he made a detour. Kentay decided to go to his place since it had been a minute since he had been there. As soon as he pulled up, one of his neighbors was in the yard. It was a man that always looked out for his neighbors, so Kentay spoke to him.

"Hey youngster… I don't think you wanna hang around here long. The laws been hot," the old man told Kentay after he walked over closer to him.

"Oh yeah… damn! I better hurry up then," Kentay replied.

"Yeah… pretty much all day everyday they riding through. They knocked on your door a couple of times, and I thought they was gonna break it down, but they ended up leaving," his neighbor told him. Kentay stood there wondering what the fuck else could go wrong while shaking his head. He told his neighbor thanks, went inside and checked on things, and then left within twenty minutes and headed to the condo he had purchased for Ashanti.

Twenty minutes later, Kentay was walking into the condo. He kicked off his shoes at the door and headed towards the back. When he got to the baby's door, he paused. After standing there for about five minutes in silence, he twisted the knob and opened the door. Walking over to the crib, he picked up one of the bears and held it tightly. No longer being able to control his emotions, Kentay fell to the floor in tears. All of the emotions he tried to keep tugged away poured out of him like a flowing river. Kentay finally pried himself up off of the floor after a little over an hour. He went and grabbed some clothes for the next day and headed out. When he pulled up at Mrs. Tina's house, he was about to text Ashanti but just got out and knocked on the door instead. The door opened up after a few moments and Tina stood to the side and let Kentay in. Ashanti was sleep when he walked into her room, so he undressed, got in bed with her and held her for the rest of the night.

***

The next morning, when Ashanti began to stir, Kentay held her tighter.

"Please don't leave me baby," he told her sweetly.

"I'm not sure I can take you having a baby with Raven and our baby died," Ashanti answered honestly without facing him.

"We can still make it. If that baby is mine, I will take care of her but that's it. That Raven shit was a mistake that I wish I could take back," he honestly explained to her.

"It's not as simple as you make it seem Tay. We have a baby to bury right now. I don't even care to think about anything else right now," Ashanti said while slowly getting up from the bed. Kentay quickly hopped up to help her. "It took this to happen for you to be attentive. That's really sad," Ashanti said and walked into the bathroom. Tay was so used to her giving in to him that he didn't know what to do. The song *When A Woman's Fed Up* popped into his head, he couldn't help but to shake his head.

"Damn, Kellz was right!"

Later on that evening, Kentay decided to leave and give Ashanti some space. The graveside ceremony was short and sweet and Ashanti only wanted her mom, Kentay, Aaliyah, Slick, and the pastor in attendance so that's what Kentay made happen. They briefly talked afterwards and he filled her in on the situation with the baby, Kendra. He didn't expect her to be sympathetic, but he wanted her to know everything that was going on. Deep down, he knew that Ashanti was slipping away but he vowed to do any and everything to possible to make their relationship work. His mind was in overload with plans to make things solid. Kentay's phone rang, and he noticed that it was one of his out of state partners who didn't call often. He was a little confused on why he would be calling, but he answered the call anyway.

"What's up?" he answered.

"We got a situation," the caller said.

"Speak on it," Tay retorted.

"I got something that I know traces back to you. When can we meet up?" ole boy inquired.

"Can you leave and meet me in Birmingham now?" Kentay asked.

"Yep. On my way," the caller replied.

"Bet," Tay replied and ended the call. He made a call to Slick and told him to meet him at one of the spots so that they could take a ride. Slick agreed and thirty minutes later they were on the road. Kentay knew what the call was about, and he was anxious to get a name. That was the call he had been waiting on to find out exactly who had crossed him. Him and Slick headed to their destination with their minds full of thoughts.

"If this is who I think it is, this shit getting handled tonight," Tay said, finally breaking the silence.

"You know I'm wit it. I just canceled that fight for the night so we can concentrate on this," Slick replied.

"We'll make up for that loss. This shit right here is imperative," Kentay stated.

"Damn right," Slick agreed while rubbing his hands together. "Got damn right," he continued and then pulled some Kush from out of the glove compartment, lit it up, and passed it to his homie after he hit a few times while they were on their way.

***

"I been thinking about bumping you up man. Shit been crazy as fuck, but don't think I haven't noticed all of the hard work you been putting in," Kentay said to one of his workers while sitting at the trap in Rock Hill.

"Word... I been tryna go hard. I know a lot of shit been going on and I been in these streets tryna keep shit smooth for ya boss man," Dro replied.

"I appreciate that and that's why I gotta reward you man," Tay responded.

The night before, Kentay and Slick made it back too late to handle any business, but they were up bright and early the next day taking care of business. It didn't take much to get Dro to the trap after Kentay hit him up offering to reward him. He showed up ahead of time with a smile on his face, and it took everything in Kentay to stick to the plan. While Slick stood at the front entrance, Kentay stood and walked to the back room.

"I'll be right back," he said and kept walking without looking back.

When Kentay walked back in the room and sat the bricks down on the table, Dro's eyes got wide as fuck.

"Don't you move a muthafuckin' inch nigga," Kentay said with his gun pointed directly at Dro's head when he shifted a little.

"I can explain man," Dro said without stuttering. Kentay gave him credit for looking him in the eyes while thinking of a lie, but no matter what he said, it was over with for him.

"Twan…" Dro started saying but Kentay cut him off.

"Nigga you just confirmed that you was wit that nigga at the trap in Blackjack by calling his name," Tay spewed. "First of all, I can't believe you had the audacity to break in the trap and steal, but I really can't believe what you did to my girl. Those bricks she gave you were dummy bricks, and that cash was fake. You wondered why I wasn't tripping on finding out who the snake was. Well I always knew that it would be revealed. I got muthafuckin eyes and ears everywhere. The nigga you hit up in Atlanta, Peanut, he's a partner of mine," Tay continued speaking.

When he walked towards Dro, he circled him and looked down on him like a bitch. He wasn't worried about him having a gun because he knew exactly where he kept it. Taking the butt of his gun, Kentay hit Dro in the nose causing blood to spew out immediately. When Dro bent down, Slick walked over and took his gun out of his pocket. Kentay pistol whipped Dro while talking shit until his face was unrecognizable. Dro kept calling Tay's name over and over until Kentay finally put a bullet in his head, silencing him forever. The body was disposed of by the clean-up crew. Unbeknownst to them, neither Tay nor Slick had any idea that Dro had been wired because they never checked or looked at his body after he was dead.

Chapter Twenty-Seven

October 18th was a day that Ashanti would never forget. It had been exactly one month since she lost her baby, and she was finally getting back into the swing of things after shutting everyone out. The only thing she did was go to class, work, and then back to her condo when she didn't feel like making the long drive to her mom's house. All of her social media accounts were deactivated, and her phone was on do not disturb pretty much all day, every day. Kentay had been very attentive to her needs, but in her eyes, it was a little too late for that. One part of her wanted to make the relationship work because of everything that she had invested, but another part of her wanted to be free from him. The fear of starting over was constantly on her mind, and it was the one thing that made her feel like she was at a dead end with nowhere to go.

After class, Aaliyah caught up with Ashanti as soon as she walked outside.

"How long are you going to shut everybody out? Ahmad is going crazy worrying about you, and you only talk to me briefly about schoolwork," Aaliyah said but Ashanti kept walking. "Ashanti I can't say I know how you feel because I don't. But, I do know that you're vibrant, and you can overcome anything. Don't let this situation make you bitter," Aaliyah begged while grabbing Ashanti's arm and forcing her to stop walking.

"You're right. I don't even know why I'm tripping. I wasn't even gonna keep the baby in the beginning but now look what happened," Ashanti said with her eyes starting to tear up.

"Don't beat yourself up like that. That had nothing to do with it sweetie. Some shit, most shit in life just happens, and we have no control over it and don't even know the reasons why. It could have happened so you won't have any connections with Kentay. Who knows," Liyah stated, trying to get Shanti to see another perspective.

"That could be true, but everything is so complicated. I don't wanna just jump from Kentay to Ahmad. And please believe me, Tay ain't gonna just let me walk away easily. He'll give me my space, but there will be hell once he finds out I'm even interested in someone else," Ashanti expressed her feelings to Liyah.

They started back walking because the wind had started to blow, and it was cold outside. It was the last day of classes before the Thanksgiving break. They were looking forward to a week out of class and then basically coming back to take finals and be out of school for over a month until the next year.

"It's all gonna work out Shanti. Just search your heart and do what's best for you no matter what anyone else says. People who genuinely love you only want the best for you. And you're looking great girl. You been working out on the low?" Aaliyah said as they were passing by the Mitchell Memorial Library.

"Thank you Liyah. We haven't even known each other that long, but it feels like an eternity already. You always know exactly what to say. And nah I haven't been working out, but I think I wanna join that new gym that's down by Total Look, where the bowling alley was. Just to get active and help manage my stress," Ashanti replied.

"I know someone who would love to work out with you… and there he is right there," Liyah said while smiling.

Before Ashanti could respond, she bumped right into Ahmad.

"I'm sorry," Ashanti told him and dropped her eyes to the ground. Ahmad lifted her chin up and stared into her eyes.

"I know you been dealing wit some serious shit, but all I need is a text saying that you're okay. Don't have a nigga out here worried because I been thinking bout doing some crazy shit like popping up," he told her.

"I know… I know… I'm really sorry. Aaliyah been on my ass all day about it. I'm gonna do better, but how have you been?" Ashanti asked while blushing.

"I'm gonna walk over to the Union. Come over when y'all are done," Liyah interrupted and walked off while smiling. Ashanti didn't know that Aaliyah had purposely led her into Ahmad's path. He had tried to catch her several times after class, but she never walked the same way anymore, so he reached out to Aaliyah because he needed to see Ashanti.

"Okay... I'll be over there in a few," Ashanti called out to her. "But back to you... how have you been? How's basketball going?" Shanti asked after directing her attention back to Ahmad.

"It's all going great... I'll probably enter the draft next year. But on the real, I been worried about you," Ahmad told her sincerely. Ashanti couldn't help but to smile, but then sadness washed over her face when his words about entering the draft registered in her mind.

"What's wrong?" Ahmad inquired.

"You entering the draft... bittersweet, but I'm happy for you," Ashanti replied.

"You coming with me," Ahmad said while laughing but he was dead serious. "It's really good to see you and that beautiful smile of yours," Ahmad continued and grabbed Ashanti's hand to head toward the union.

"It's good to see you too. Really good," Ashanti replied. There was an awkward silence before Ashanti spoke again. "So when is your next basketball game?" she asked him already knowing the answer but she loved seeing his face light up when she talked about the sport he loved so much.

"We don't play again until the week after the break. It's up in Oxford so I won't make you come," he told her. "But I have been missing my good luck charm," he continued. Ashanti playfully hit him and told him that she would be at the next home game for sure. When he mentioned Oxford, she couldn't help but to think about Kya and how much they had grown apart since and that's where she was going to school. Ashanti had reached out to her through text messages and even phone calls, but she never replied so she finally just gave up. It hurt Ashanti that she couldn't didn't have her friend there during her time of need, but Aaliyah stepped in made everything better.

"What's on your mind?" Ahmad asked after he noticed her change in mood.

"I was just thinking about my friend, well I guess ex friend Kya that's up at Ole Miss," Ashanti replied and filled him in on the story. Ahmad told her that some friends are with you for a reason, some for a season, and others are there for a lifetime and never get them mixed up because it will cause you more than a little bit of pain.

Once they made it to the union, they talked for a few more minutes before Ahmad opened the door for Ashanti to walk in first. As soon as they walked in, all eyes were on them.

"You might as well get used to the spotlight baby. You know I plan on making you mine as soon as the time is right," Ahmad playfully told Shanti after noticing the look on her face.

"You think I can get used to all these hoes staring? My patience ain't what it used to be," Ashanti joked.

"Yeah, you ain't gon have shit to worry bout. They can look but I guarantee you they won't touch," he sincerely replied. They made it over to Aaliyah, and she was finishing up with a chicken sandwich.

"I thought y'all lovebirds had ran off and eloped or some shit," she said after wiping some mayonnaise from the side of her mouth.

"Not yet, but Ima kidnap her one day and won't be no eloping unless that's what she wants," Ahmad replied while smirking making Ashanti blush yet again. "But let me run on to the gym… have your phone on later," he instructed while facing Ashanti. Ashanti shocked herself by reaching out to him and pulling him in for a hug. She inhaled his scent and didn't want to let go. From his reaction, she could tell that he didn't want to either by the grip he had on her. After they finally broke from each other's embrace, Ahmad headed to the gym while Ashanti and Aaliyah headed to their last two classes of the day. They made plans to hook up and just hang out over the break as Ashanti promised to do better. She was off work for the day and planned on going straight home to take a nap because she was tired.

***

Ashanti hopped into her Range Rover after class was over and went to Penn's and ordered a shrimp po'boy with fries and a sprite before heading home. She was glad her last class got canceled so she was an hour ahead of schedule. Her plans were to eat as soon as she walked in and crawl under the covers and take a much needed nap. When Ashanti pulled into her complex and drove around towards her building, she saw Tay's truck and wondered what he was doing there that time of day. She was so used to him being out handling business. Normally, he wouldn't tell her about what was going on in the streets. But a couple of weeks ago, he told her about how one of his boys had backstabbed him and let her know that he was the one who robbed her. He didn't have to tell her what happened next because she already knew. Ashanti knew all of that came with the territory, but it wasn't anything that she wanted to or would ever get used to.

When Ashanti pulled out her key to unlock the door, it opened and Kentay was standing there smiling from ear to ear.

"You're early babe… I was just bout to order some food. I wasn't even gon' act like I cooked," he told her and then his eyes went down to her bag of food.

"I figured you would be gone by the time I got out of class," Shanti replied.

"I just been sitting and thinking all day and wanted to spend some time with you," Kentay replied and grabbed Ashanti's food and bag out of her hands. When he grabbed her food from her left hand, he noticed that she wasn't wearing her ring. "Your fingers still swollen?" he asked while walking off.

"I could lie and say yes, but I honestly I just haven't thought to put it back on," Shanti replied while walking towards the table where he was taking her food. "You want me to go and get you something to eat?" she offered, trying to change the subject.

"Nah babe, I'm good," he replied. Ashanti sat down and wondered when the real Kentay was going to show up because the one before her was being too calm.

"Eat your food before it gets cold," he prompted her. As soon as he said it, Ashanti's stomach started growling again so she dug right in. "How are your classes going?" Tay inquired.

"Pretty good. I have four A's and one B so I can't complain. As long as I do well on my finals I'll be happy," Ashanti replied while dipping a shrimp in some cocktail sauce.

"That's great. I'm really proud of you. You're not just any girl to me. The females I dealt with in the past would just sit at home and live off of what I do, but you have ambition and I love that about you," Kentay told her.

"Thank you Tay, but where is all of this coming from?" Shanti asked.

"I'm just saying. I notice a lot but I don't say shit. I'm really tryna do better though. I've done a bunch of bullshit in my past, some shit that might even catch up wit me, but I'm tryna be straight up wit you from here out," Kentay told her.

"Do you honestly think that everything that has happened is repairable? I can't even open the door to that room for the fear of breaking down at the sight of all the baby stuff. I know I can't totally blame you for everything, because I've always just put up with your shit. However, this Raven and the baby deal is just too much. Without a test, I can tell you know that baby is yours. And as much I don't like her ass, I'm pretty sure she needs you," Ashanti expressed some of her feelings after sitting there thinking for a while. She lost her appetite and tears started forming in her eyes, so she got up from the table and headed to the master bedroom.

"Baby… I'm doing everything I can to make it work. Please work with me. Don't give up on us. You see I been begging like a lil bitch," Tay said while laughing and trying to break the ice.

"My mind is just all over the place right now. I just wanna go wit the flow, live my life, and see what happens," Shanti told him while kicking off her shoes and changing into a tank top.

"Have you met someone else?" Tay asked walking towards the bed while she was climbing in.

"What if I have?" Ashanti asked him.

"Shanti don't play wit me. I can't even deal wit the fuckin' thought. Just forget I asked, but you gon' always be mine," Tay said while stripping and getting in the bed with her.

"They say if you love something you gotta let it go, and if it comes back then it means so much more," Ashanti said thinking about Heather Headley's song *In My Mind*.

"Fuck all that," Tay replied and pulled Ashanti close to him. He kissed her sensually. Ashanti tried to pull away at first, but before long she yielded to him. She hadn't had sex since before losing the baby and his kisses had her wet within a few moments. Kentay pulled her panties off while kissing her. Since she had taken her bra off already, her breasts were already free and he gave them some much needed attention. Ashanti knew that her moans were turning Kentay on because he seemed to be enjoying the foreplay more than her. By the time he reached her throbbing clit, she had already came once. He ate her so good that she was ready to return the favor, but he entered her slowly before she could move a muscle.

"Ahhh," they said in unison.

"Damn bae, I been missing this good pussy. Don't ever give my pussy away," Kentay groaned while stroking her. Ashanti was too caught up in the moment to reply. The two of them made love into the night like it was their last time.

Chapter Twenty-Eight

Raven called Jason repeatedly, but he never answered her calls. She texted him more than she called and all of the messages went unanswered. With not knowing exactly where her baby was along with Kentay not being there to comfort her, Raven was sinking into a deep depression. She found herself drinking for breakfast, lunch, and dinner. Banging on the door woke Raven up from her drunken state.

BOOM BOOM BOOM!!

BOOM BOOM BOOM!!

"I'm cominnggg" Raven slurred after dragging herself up from the couch.

"What the fuck is wrong wit you?" Kentay fumed after Raven opened the door. Raven stumbled to the side to let him in, but he stood just stood in place staring at her. "This ain't no social visit. Are you even looking for the baby?" Kentay inquired.

Raven started crying and fell into Tay's arms. It was clear that Kentay was hesitant to embrace her or go inside because he kept looking around and shifting from foot to foot. He reluctantly went inside when one of the neighbors walked outside. Raven cried harder in his arms and pulled him until they fell onto the loveseat that was right beside the door.

"I've been needing you!" Raven sobbed.

"I been looking all over and having people look for the type of car you said he drive, but ain't shit came up. What have the police said?" Kentay asked. Raven shifted away from him when he asked about the police.

"What? They ain't got no leads?" he asked.

"I... I haven't called the... the police," Raven stuttered.

"WHAT THE FUCK YOU MEAN?" Kentay jumped up and screamed.

"It's complicated Tay," Raven said, standing up as well.

"How complicated is it? Do you care that the baby is even missing or are you just using that as an excuse to contact me twenty-four seven?" Tay asked through clenched teeth.

"I don't feel like he will hurt her," Raven timidly stated. "And I have needed you," she continued.

"When you learn to stop playing games and get the baby back, contact me so we can get a blood test. But don't fucking call or text me unless that's what it's for," Kentay said and left without saying another word or acknowledging Raven's cries. Raven picked up the bottle of Jack Daniels that was on the floor beside the couch, finished it off and plopped down on the couch. She sent Jason another text that went unanswered and wondered if it was time to get the police involved.

***

Kentay left Raven's apartment so abruptly because he wanted to choke slam her. He couldn't stand being around the police but couldn't understand the logic behind a mother not calling the police if her child had really been kidnapped. Stopping at the Shell station to get some gas, Tay's phone chimed with a text message as soon as he parked by pump number four. He read the message Ashanti sent and was confused by what it stated. Before he could reply and get clarity on her text, another one came through.

Ashanti: *Thanks for the talk. I can always depend on you.*

Ashanti: *Sorry babe, that was for Aaliyah but I clicked your name by mistake because you were on my mind.*

Kentay sat there for a few minutes in deep thought, stuck and unable to move. He told himself that Ashanti cleaned that up real quick and wondered if it was the truth. His gut was telling him that his baby had found another man, but his ego wouldn't allow him to believe it. Kentay thought about the time he heard Ashanti say someone's name in her sleep. But he couldn't tell if she had said Mark, Jamal or what. The only sound that he was sure of was the "M" but he missed the beginning. Dismissing the thoughts, he got out and pumped his gas and decided that it was all just his imagination because he knew Ashanti was a good girl.

An hour later, Tay and Slick were out in Blackjack chopping it up at the spot. The word had spread about Dro, and it seemed like everybody had a story to tell about him after the fact. Kentay had to cuss a few niggas out for not coming forth with information sooner. Hearing that he had been working with the cops had been the most disturbing news out of everything. With this new information known, Tay and Slick personally switched up their regular routines and took shit to secret locations. They still frequented the regular spots to make everything appear to be normal, but if they were to get raided, they would be good.

"Say bruh, I can't help but to feel like there's somebody else that we need to keep our eyes on more closely. I just got a gut feeling that shit still ain't right and some shit is bout to go down soon," Slick said to his boy.

"I been feeling like that too man. No way in hell Dro and Twan were in this alone. Shit still ain't adding up but I haven't caught anybody else slipping yet," Tay replied.

"Time will definitely tell, but we just gotta keep moving smarter either way it go. You remember that night at Club Kiss that you ran over somebody or something when you was leaving? I been meaning to ask you 'bout that shit because I been hearing that it was one of the city cop's son or some shit. They kept the shit a secret because he was at a club but now they saying the nigga is paralyzed.

"I remember hearing a bump when I left, but I damn shol didn't know it was a body," Tay said after thinking back for a minute.

"You haven't been driving that truck lately and I wouldn't if I was you," Slick advised him.

"I'll keep that in mind. Good looking out," Kentay agreed.

"No doubt," Slick said and finished off his Corona. They finished handling business and then decided to head their separate ways until the next day.

The next morning, Kentay woke up and nudged Ashanti. She rolled over and wiped the sleep out of her eyes before focusing on him.

"Come on let's take a trip. We ain't got away from here in a minute, and it's long overdue," Tay said as he watched her body language closely.

"Where you wanna go? You know Thanksgiving is next week and my mom is expecting me," Shanti sleeply replied.

"Let's shoot to Vegas. It's Saturday, we can stay like two or three days then come on back," Kentay told her. He could tell that Ashanti was in deep thought by the look on her face.

"Your birthday is tomorrow, you not having your party tonight?" Ashanti asked curiously.

"I'd rather spend it alone with you. Besides, I have tickets already and a suite at the MGM Grand booked. I wasn't feeling the party because too much shit going on in the streets. Sometimes I feel like my end time is near and I just wanna make the best of it," Tay told her.

"Don't talk like that. Yeah, we can go. I won't be able to gamble because I'm not twenty-one, but I guess we can make the best of it," Ashanti replied, finally smiling a little.

"Don't you worry about all that. I got that covered," Tay said and pulled her in close for a kiss. "Come on… let's hop in the shower. We don't even need bags, everything is straight," Kentay told Ashanti and pulled her up. When he left from kicking it with Slick the day before, he called his travel agent and had her plan everything and his only task was to get Ashanti to say yes. The flight was leaving out of the Golden Triangle Airport at eleven, so they had four hours before the departure, which was fine since they were only twenty minutes away. So far, everything was working out just the way he envisioned and hoped the rest of his plans played out the same.

At two o'clock West Coast time, they were landing at McCarran International in Las Vegas, Nevada. The connecting flight they had in Atlanta was only forty minutes, and they were right back in the air after the thirty-five minute flight from Mississippi.

"So what about our clothes and stuff?" Ashanti asked while they were walking off of the plane.

"No worries babe... I got it," Kentay replied and kissed her hand after lifting it up to his mouth. When they walked out of the airport, Kentay spotted the stretch Hummer he had rented with a man standing beside it holding a sign with his last name. "This way," he told Ashanti and headed that way.

They were seated and Kentay didn't waste any time popping open the bottle of champagne that was in the bucket of ice. He poured both of them a glass and made a toast.

"To new beginnings," he said and clinked Ashanti's glass, and they drank after she recited what he said. The ride from the airport to the hotel was only about ten minutes. After the driver stopped, he got out and opened the door for them to exit. He held out his hand to help Ashanti, but Kentay stepped up and told him he had it and then instructed the driver to park and let him know that he would call him when he was needed. Kentay paid good money to have him on standby just in case, and he expected that whether he used him or not, the driver was still getting paid.

Kentay had taken Ashanti on several trips, but it was her first trip to Vegas, and he could tell that she was loving the MGM Grand by the look on her face. He couldn't wait until they made it upstairs to their suite, so he could see the look on her face. After walking through the place for almost an hour and retrieving the room keys, they found the elevators for the west wing and headed up to the fifteenth floor. Kentay opened the door and let Ashanti walk in first as he smiled when he saw the look on her face.

"Wow! This is beautiful. Is this a honeymoon suite?" Shanti asked while walking around the enormous and exquisite room, admiring its beauty.

"I asked for the most beautiful suite here because I was bringing the most beautiful woman in the world, so it might be," Kentay smoothly replied.

"I wish your ass was this sweet all the time," Ashanti said and picked up a pillow and threw it at him.

"I'm getting there babe," he told her and kissed her on the neck. "I ain't bout to play with you. We got reservations. Go look in the closet and find something to wear for dinner," Tay told her and watched her open the closet and admire all of the clothes that had been handpicked for her.

"You went all out I see. Where we going so I'll know what to put on?" she asked.

"Some shit called Top of the World at the Stratosphere. The travel agent said it's nice as fuck so we gon see," he told her.

"Sounds good. What time is the reservation?" Ashanti inquired.

"Tonight at eight. I just wanted you to see what was in the closet to make sure you like it," Tay retorted.

"Yeah this some nice shit," she replied after pulling out a dress to wear later.

"Cool… we can just chill out and relax for a few hours then we'll get ready. Rest up because it's on and popping nonstop after we leave," Kentay said and closed his eyes to take a nap. He felt Ashanti lay down beside him and pulled her close to him.

Later on that evening, Kentay and Ashanti were both dressed in all white and were turning heads left and right throughout the hotel. The designer had done an excellent job with picking out clothes, and Kentay had to make a mental note to tip her extra. The limo was waiting at the front door as soon as they walked out. Traffic was thick, but they still made it on time for their reservations. Leading the way to the elevator, Kentay hit the roof top button once they made it and rode up in silence.

The hostess greeted them about five minutes after their arrival, and they were seated. The view was amazing. Finally, Kentay saw what all of the hype was about. Kentay ordered drinks when the waitress came and Ashanti ordered the appetizers. The waitress never asked for Ashanti's ID since Kentay placed the order. He planned on getting her sloppy drunk later that night and bringing his birthday, November 20th, in a very special way. When looking out of the windows, you could see the city of Vegas lit up. The rotation was very slow, and Ashanti pointed out one of the casinos an hour later that she saw when they first sat down. Dinner was amazing and Kentay told her that the night wasn't over and led the way back down after they demolished their dessert.

***

Ashanti woke up with banging headache. When she glanced at the clock on the nightstand, she noticed that it was 3:26.

"Is that 3:26 pm?" Ashanti said while rubbing her head.

"Bout time you woke up. Yeah it's pm," Kentay said while walking out of the bathroom and laughing.

"Damn… what in the hell happened last night? I don't even remember shit," Shanti said while attempting to get up, but she fell right back down on the bed.

"Last night was wonderful. You forgot everything? You were pretty fucked up but I thought you would remember," Kentay replied sounding a little disappointed.

"All I remember is drinking wit yo ass and you gave me a pill to take to keep from having a headache when I woke up but clearly that shit didn't work," Ashanti said, finally getting up.

"Damn babe… I wanted you to remember how we brought my birthday in," Tay hummed.

"Oh shit! Happy Birthday baby!" Shanti said and went and hugged Kentay. He swooped her up into his arms and kissed her. When he started spinning her around, she told him that she felt dizzy so he put her down. "Let me hop in the shower right quick and maybe I'll feel better," Ashanti said after a few minutes. She paused when she looked in the mirror and saw the big ass ring on her finger.

"Since you haven't been wearing the other one, I bought you a bigger and better one. I love you Shanti. I really do," Kentay said and gave her another long hug and squeezed her ass.

"I love you too Tay," Ashanti said while smiling and meaning it. At that moment, to say she was conflicted about her whole life would be an understatement. She knew that she had to get her shit together soon. Very soon. When she texted Ahmad and told him that she would be out of town with Kentay for a few days, he said he was okay, but she knew that he wasn't. *God you gotta give me a clear sign* Ashanti thought to herself and headed in the bathroom.

An hour later, they were eating at AquaKnox and enjoying each other. They talked and laughed with each other like old times and decided to gamble a little bit when they left the restaurant. While walking out, Ashanti saw a lady in a wedding dress and stopped.

"Did we watch some people get married last night?" she asked Kentay after trying to remember everything that happened.

"Yeah, you remembering everything now?" he coyly asked.

"Not much, but seeing that lady triggered something," Ashanti admitted. They left and walked on the floor where no one was checking ID, and Ashanti won five hundred dollars the first five minutes and tucked it deep into her purse. Kentay played craps while she cheered him on. Five hours later, they were both five thousand dollars richer.

On Tuesday, Ashanti and Kentay got dressed and met the limo driver downstairs at 9:00 sharp so that he could take them to the airport. They both agreed that the spontaneous trip was awesome and one of the best that they had taken. Kentay promised to do better and make her the happiest woman on earth. Ashanti hoped that he really meant it but silently prayed for a sign from God to let her know what she needed to do because she didn't want to continue stringing Ahmad along.

Chapter Twenty-Nine

Kya was beyond elated to be going home for the Thanksgiving holidays. Blow tried to make her stay with him, but she told him that it was imperative that she went home to visit her mom. She hadn't been home since school started, and her mom had been sick a lot lately. She added the last part to gain sympathy and to make keep him from putting his hands on her knowing that she would be going home. It worked in her favor because he was sweet for the days leading up to break. Kya played the role that she would love and miss him to the tee while being forced to suck his toddler dick.

On Saturday morning, Kya was on her way home, and she couldn't be happier. She wanted to call Ashanti but decided that she would just surprise her once she made it. Planning on that being her first stop, she headed towards Starkville. Amanda called Kya while she was driving and they talked for most of the ride while she was headed home herself. They made plans to link up during the holidays if time permitted. The semester was going great for both of them and despite Kya's circumstances, she still managed to keep her grades good, and she was happy about it.

An hour and a half later, Kya was parking at Carpenter Place, and shortly afterwards, she was knocking on Ashanti's door. When no one came after a few minutes, Kya pulled her phone out of her pocket and dialed Ashanti's number, but it went straight to voicemail.

"Damn... guess I'll try again next week," Kya said to herself while walking back to her car. As soon as Kya hopped in her car, her phone rang. When she looked at the name on the screen, she was shocked as hell, but she answered the call anyway.

"Hello," Kya spoke.

"I know I'm the last person you thought would be calling, but I need someone to talk to," the caller said. Hearing the sadness in the voice, Kya decided to listen to the rest of the call and then said that she was on her way.

Fifteen minutes later, she turned in The Links and parked. When the door opened, Kya was taken back at Raven's look.

"Raven… what the fuck? Have you been… bitch, go get your ass in the shower and then we can talk," Kya adamantly stated.

"Same ole smart mouth Kya," Raven replied while rolling her eyes.

"I'm for real… I'll wait a few minutes but I know a damn shower should help you feel a little better," Kya retorted. Raven told Kya that she would be back shortly and then disappeared to the back.

Kya walked around Raven's living room not taking in the smell of alcohol and looking at junk everywhere. Raven never told her what the issue was over the phone. She only said that it was very important so Kya finally agreed to come over. Since she heard the shower water still running, she walked to one of the rooms and noticed the baby crib was gone along with other items and wondered where the baby was. When the water stopped, Kya went back to the living room and impatiently waited for Raven's return.

"You were right, that shower did help me feel better, but it doesn't help my problems," Raven said walking back into the room where Kya was waiting about five minutes after Kya walked back in.

"Where's the baby?" Kya asked, getting straight to the point. Raven sighed and filled Kya in on everything that had been going on, and Kya stood there in awe while listening to her. By the time Raven finished talking, Kya felt sorry for her but still wondered why she was confiding in her.

"I really hate that all of this happened, but I'm not sure what you want me to do," Kya stated after Raven was finally done talking.

"I really don't know. I just needed someone to talk to," Raven sadly replied.

Kya stood there in deep thought while thinking about her own bullshit and her distant relationship with Ashanti. She could tell that Raven pretty much wanted her back as a friend, but she knew that wouldn't sit too well with Ashanti considering the circumstances. After pacing back and forth for what seemed like an eternity, Kya finally spoke.

"Since you still haven't called the police, track Jason's phone. That shouldn't be hard to do, and you can pull up a location. On all that other stuff, give me some time to think about it and I'll get back with you," Kya said and left shortly afterwards.

While driving and constantly thinking, Kya made her way down highways 82 headed home. She hadn't traveled the road in a minute, but she could still drive it with her eyes closed because it was so familiar to her. Pulling into the driveway, Kya noticed that her mom was home and she hoped that she was in a good mood. If not, she knew that they would be going back and forth with each other like always. After unlocking the door, Kya walked inside and found her mother on the couch asleep with an empty Smirnoff bottle beside her and the smell of marijuana lingering throughout the living room. Instead of bothering her, Kya headed to her room and laid across the bed in deep thought. Her mother never told her who her dad was and every time she asked, she got cussed out. Kya always felt like whoever her dad was must have been the reason her mom turned to drugs and alcohol. She figured it was because she couldn't have him or something, but whatever it was she really wished that her mom would snap out of it.

***

The day before Thanksgiving, Kya was out getting last minute items for her mom to cook dinner. Wal-Mart was the last place she wanted to be, but since it was a one stop shop store, that was where she went. Picking up some cranberry sauce, Hawaiian rolls, and some drinks, Kya decided that she wanted something sweet for the night so she walked to the back so that she could grab some chocolate chip cookies to bake. Once they were in her basket, she turned to leave and bumped into someone.

"Oh shit, I'm so sorry… I didn't even," she started saying and then locked eyes with Ashanti. "Shanti," Kya said and then her eyes went down to her stomach.

"Kya," Ashanti bluntly stated.

"You had the baby already? When? Why didn't…" she started asking questions but cut them off once she realized that Ashanti had been in fact reaching out to her, but she was the one who never called or texted back. "I'm sorry. I just…" Kya said before Ashanti cut her off.

"No need to be sorry Kya. We promised to never grow apart but sometimes shit just happens right? I've called and texted you more times than I can remember, but you never even replied. Yes I had my baby, but he died. I needed you, but you showed me that you weren't a real friend during my time of need. In fact, in one message, I told you that I needed you, but you ignored that message too. Did you change your number and not tell me? Don't even answer that. I did nothing but love you and Raven like the sisters I never had, but y'all were always low key jealous, and I don't even care to know why anymore. I wish you the best in life, but this friendship is over," Ashanti said and walked off. After Shanti walked off, Kya stood there speechless. She wanted to call out to her but she just let Ashanti walk out of her life because she knew that every word Ashanti spoke was true.

Chapter Thirty

"The passive movement of particles from an area of high concentration to low concentration. This happens along a concentration gradient?" Aaliyah asked while her and Ashanti were quizzing each other on a biology exam.

"Diffusion," Ashanti replied while playing with her phone.

"You getting all of these answers right, but your mind shol ain't on this shit," Liyah stated. "What's wrong?" she continued. Ashanti sighed, put her phone down and then started talking.

"Do you remember me talking about Kya? I'm sure you do. Well I ran into her at Wal-Mart the day before Thanksgiving, and I been in my feelings ever since. It's like she basically said fuck me. I told her how I felt and walked off, thinking she was gonna stop me, but nope. She didn't say shit," Ashanti vented and then sighed again. After a few moments of silence, Shanti gave Liyah the story word for word and asked her if she was in the wrong.

"I can't say you were in the wrong at all, but I can tell that it's bothering you. Maybe you should reach out one more time since it's on your mind," Liyah stated.

"Why the hell would I do that? You know how many times I called and texted her and got no reply?" Ashanti stated becoming mad.

"Okay… okay, I was just saying," Aaliyah replied while laughing and trying to make the light of the conversation.

"I don't feel like I was wrong. I'm not gonna keep dwelling on the shit though. It is what it is," Ashanti said while picking her phone back up.

"You ready to ace this exam?" Aaliyah asked her.

"Yep… and then I want you to ride with me somewhere later," Ashanti said while smiling.

"I bet I can guess where. You tryna surprise somebody and be their good luck charm tonight?" Liyah inquired while smirking.

"Maybe I am," Ashanti answered and began blushing.

"I'm down… and on the real, somebody gonna come through and scoop Ahmad up if you don't claim him. I heard he been turning all his lil jump offs down and you ain't even giving him none," Aaliyah said to her friend.

"Ima get this shit together soon, but I don't wanna be jumping from one nigga to the next," Ashanti replied as they walked toward Harned Hall.

"Everyone situation is different Shanti. I thought you were getting rid of Kentay, but ever since that Vegas trip, y'all seem to be doing better. I'm not telling you what to do, all I'm saying is Ahmad won't be single forever girl," Aaliyah stated.

"I know… I've been praying for a sign. I'm going to the game tonight though and that's all that matters right now," Ashanti replied right before they walked into class.

***

Later on that night, after acing their exams, Ashanti and Aaliyah were on their way to Oxford to surprise Ahmad at his basketball game. Ashanti had her Apple Music on Jennifer Hudson and when *If This Isn't Love* came on she sang her heart out.

If this isn't love, tell me what it is…

cause I could be dreaming or just plain crazy…

if this isn't love tell me what it is, cause I never felt like this baby!

"You gon' sing that to Ahmad later?" Aaliyah asked while laughing and cutting Ashanti's mini concert short.

"You just stay with the jokes I see," Ashanti replied while playfully rolling her eyes. They both sang, laughed, joked, and talked for the rest of ride until they pulled up on Ole Miss Campus at 6:15, forty-five minutes before the game was scheduled to start.

"Did these folks up here ever decide if they were rebels, black bears or land sharks?" Aaliyah asked and they both burst out laughing.

"Hell if I know or even care. That says a lot about the school anyway...dumb asses," Ashanti replied and they both laughed again and finally got out and headed inside.

By the time they made it in and got seated, it was 6:45. They could have been sitting down before then, but Aaliyah wanted some popcorn and a Coke from the concession stand, and Ashanti didn't fuss because she wanted some nachos and something to drink herself. As soon as they sat down behind the visitor's bench, the basketball team ran out and the crowd started booing them like crazy.

"These hoes are rude as fuck up here," Ashanti stated loudly while looking around and rolling her eyes. Aaliyah agreed with her and gave a few people some death stares of her own. When Ashanti turned back toward the court, she locked eyes with Ahmad and he smiled from ear to ear, just like she was doing.

Ahmad did his thing on the court, and his partner Seth was making a statement too. At halftime, the game was pretty close with MSU only leading 55-51. Midway through the third quarter, the Bulldogs started to pull off which resulted in a blowout with the final score being 105-71 As soon as Ahmad was done talking to teammates and shaking hands, a news reporter stopped him for an interview. Ashanti saw that he kept glancing her way and she smiled, assuring him that she wasn't going anywhere. Fifteen minutes later, he was headed her way, but he didn't make it far before some light skinned chick stopped him and spoke while smiling. Ahmad was nice to her, and Ashanti finally noticed that he was near her. She couldn't help but to feel some type of way about the girl and wondered exactly who she was, even though deep down she felt like she had no right to ask.

"My good luck charm made it!" Ahmad said and picked Ashanti up and gave her a bear hug. In that moment, she told herself to fuck that girl she just saw and enjoy her moment.

"Yeah I decided to come on up since you think I can only come to home games," Ashanti replied while smiling.

They talked for a few minutes and then Seth walked up. Ahmad introduced him to Aaliyah, and they seemed to hit it off instantly. The coaches had to call them to the locker room because it was time to leave. Ashanti and Aaliyah told the guys great game again and promised to celebrate with them when it was convenient for everyone. Ashanti watched Ahmad walk off and caught him looking back at her again. She blew him a kiss and when she turned to leave, she saw the same girl who had stopped him watching her every move. Ashanti was about to tell Aaliyah to look at the girl, but she saw her looking in that direction before she could open her mouth.

"I told you… you better snatch that man up because these hoes are on the prowl," Aaliyah said while they were walking off.

"Damn… you ain't lying!" Ashanti replied out loud while in deep thought.

Chapter Thirty-One

"Well Miss Kya Taylor, I must say that you buckled down after a rough start and conquered these nineteen hours like a pro. The two online winter break classes that you signed up for start in three days, are you ready?" Kya's counselor asked her while they planning her next schedule.

"Yes ma'am. I get to party for two days and then it's back to business," Kya answered.

"Just stay focused and you'll definitely obtain your goal. I don't even allow most freshmen to take this route, but you were pretty determined and I do see your ambition," the counselor while finalizing Kya's winter break and spring schedules.

"Thank you so much. I'll be back to visit in January and show you these A's again," Kya said as she got up to leave. They said their goodbyes, and Kya was feeling more confident than before. "Stay focused Kya. You can do it," she said to herself while walking out of the Academic Advising building.

Even though Kya was done with class momentarily, she didn't plan on leaving Oxford. Part of it was for her benefit so that she could have fun, but the most part was because of Blow and his controlling ways. She was so happy that he was out of town for a few days, and she was ready to kick back and party with Amanda later that night. Kya rode through McDonald's drive thru and ordered a number one with extra mac sauce, a sprite to drink, and a caramel sundae with extra nuts. Her initial plan was to take it to the room to eat while watching TV, but everything was gone before she made it back to her room.

Amanda was laying on her bed eating pizza and wings and watching *The Player's Club*. Kya walked in on the part when Diamond was beating the fuck out of Ronnie in the dressing room.

"What you wearing tonight?" Kya asked her friend when she plopped down in her bed.

"I don't even know. You wanna run to Tupelo and go to the mall?" Amanda asked.

"Yeah that's cool wit me. I think I wanna find a dress to wear instead of the tights I had in mind anyway," Kya replied.

Thirty minutes later, they were on their way to the mall.

"You didn't come to Memphis over the Thanksgiving break so you gotta come this time. I know a lot of people that work on Beale Street, and we can even get drinks without ID," Amanda stated elatedly.

"I definitely gotta come. The two classes I'm taking over the break are easy so I won't be stressed," Kya responded.

"I can't believe you taking all these classes. Yo ass really tryna finish up I see," Amanda said.

"Girl yeah. I plan on working for a year a two and then going back to become a Nurse Practitioner. I wanna be successful on my own instead of having a man to make shit happen for me," Kya retorted.

"Are you throwing shade at your old friend again? I thought she was in school too," Amanda said.

"I'm just saying," Kya mumbled and turned the radio up.

The rest of the ride was filled with music and Kya and her thoughts. She wanted to reach out to Ashanti, but her pride wouldn't let her. Telling herself that the friendship wasn't meant to last and that was sent to her Amanda by God was how she coped with everything. When Amanda parked at the Mall at Barnes Crossing, they got out and the first store they went inside of was Rainbow. Kya and Amanda both found outfits that they liked but decided to go look on the racks at Charlotte Russe before purchasing them. After looking there and also browsing in Charming Charlie's for accessories, and a couple of other stores, they made their way back to Rainbow. Before they walked out, Kya noticed a familiar face and sucked her teeth. The girl heard her and looked her up and down like she wanted to fuck her up on visual. However, she was holding the hand of a child that appeared to be two or three years old. Locking eyes with the child, Kya knew without a doubt that Blow was the father of that little boy.

"Yeah this is Blow's son you bitch. Can you stare any harder?" the girl who Kya had the altercation with when she first met Blow at the store spat.

"Bitch, he ain't here to save you today. You better keep it moving," Kya replied while taking a step closer towards the woman. Amanda stepped in between them to diffuse the situation.

"You ain't even worth me going to jail over, but please believe I'll catch you in the streets. Better be tryna save your energy for them ass whoopings Blow be putting on you because I know it's going down by now," the lady said and walked off like she had just told Rock T's joke of the day.

"That bitch is as delusional as Blow," Kya before walking into Rainbow with Amanda close behind her so that they could purchase their outfits and leave.

***

Kya looked at herself in the mirror and admired her body in the white bodycon dress she had bought and her red pumps and did a spin. She thought about Blow and pulled her dress down a little, but then it clicked that he was gone so she said fuck it and pulled it back up. After double checking her makeup, she looked at Amanda rocking an all-black mini dress and heels and gave her the thumbs up. They took a few selfies for Snap Chat and Instagram and then headed out. They planned on doing a little club hopping and the first place they stopped by was The Green Roof Lounge to get a few free drinks and then headed on to Night Life after about an hour. The party was on point, and Kya was the life of the party. She had no idea what all was mixed in the punch, but she was on cup number ten in less than an hour after arriving. Dancing on top of tables, people started throwing money at Kya, and she was enjoying the moment. Videos were being made and posted on every social media site imaginable, and when a few people from class recognized who Kya was, they tagged her.

"Come with me to the bathroom," Kya told Amanda, pulling her away from her dance partner.

"I'm so glad you're enjoying yourself. Yo ass all over social media. Magic City gon be contacting you soon," Amanda said while laughing.

"I'll shol go and make that money too," Kya replied and stopped and started twerking. Another crowd started forming around her, and she was the center of attention once again. When *Back That Azz Up* by Juvenile came on, Kya forgot all about going to the bathroom and began twerking even harder. The crowd was cheering her on while singing the lyrics to the throwback song that everybody and their mama knew.

Now now now now now

After you back it up, then stop

Then wha wha what drop it like it's hot

Now after you back it up, then stop

Now, wha wha what drop it like it's hot

C-M-B make you drop it like it's hot

Drop it like it's hot, drop it like it's hot

Drop it like it's hot. Drop it like it's hot!

As soon as the song ended and Kya stopped the dancing, the guy who was grinding on her while they were dancing tried to pull her to the side. The crowd started splitting because someone was coming through and rumbling hard. Kya didn't know what happened because she blacked out after feeling excruciating pain to her face.

***

An hour later, Kya woke up in more pain and could barely move. As soon as she tried to move, she heard that voice that she had grown to hate.

"Wake up and take this beat down like the hoe you was being. I don't like putting my hands on you, but you make me do this shit," Blow fumed and kicked Kya in the side.

"Owww... stop. Please... please stop," Kya begged through her cries.

"Get up and get in the bed," Blow yelled. It was then that Kya realized she was at Blow's house. She saw her purse and cell phone on the floor beside her, but decided that it would probably be best not to touch it at the moment. She was glad that he grabbed it instead of leaving it and prayed that she could get back to it later. Moving slowly as a turtle, Kya made her way up and around to the side of the bed. Her body felt like she had been run over by a hundred dump trucks. Her face was numb, and she knew that Blow had beaten the fuck out of her while she was unconscious.

Kya finally climbed in the bed and through her half shut eyes, she saw Blow undressing and knew what time it was. *I wish he would just kill me* she thought to herself. Blow climbed into the bed and Kya cringed. She thought that he was going to make her suck his little dick again, but surprisingly, he just tried to put it inside of her.

"Moan bitch!" he groaned and Kya put on the performance that she had gotten so used to displaying, boosting his ego. Three minutes later, Blow was done. He laid next to her on the bed and pulled Kya close to him and was snoring within minutes.

She laid there awake for about three hours straight, not moving while wondering if she had enough strength to get to her purse. Moving a little bit, Blow stirred and sleepily asked her where she was going.

"To the bathroom," Kya weakly replied.

"Come right back," he said with his eyes still closed and let her go. Kya made her way to the side of the bed and put her feet down. A pain shot up her right side that caused her to moan and hold her breath, but when it stopped she proceeded. In her mind, all she wanted to do was get to her purse. It took five long minutes for Kya to grab her phone and purse and make it to the bathroom.

When she made it inside of the bathroom, she locked the door behind her and opened her purse. Tears began to flow down her cheeks when she noticed that the gun she had purchased was no longer in there. Looking up and staring in the mirror, Kya didn't even recognize the woman that was staring back at her. Her face was swollen and visible black and blue marks covered it. Standing there, she wondered what she could do to get rid of Blow once and for all. Thinking about the gun that he always kept under his pillow, Kya wrecked her brain trying to figure out a way to retrieve it.

Her feet led her to the kitchen, and before she even knew what was going on, she was back in the bedroom holding a black cast iron skillet over Blow's head. As soon as he opened his eyes, she brought both of her arms down with force and hit him right in the middle of the face. Not stopping with one hit, she beat him until she was completely out of breath. Blood was splattered everywhere. Blow looked dead, but that didn't stop Kya was grabbing the gun from under his pillow. Pacing the floor, she wondered if she could really shoot him. When thoughts of all of the beatings flooded her mind, she walked over to him and shot him one time. Not knowing exactly where the bullet landed, she fell to the floor crying and a sense of peace instantly washed over her.

When Kya grabbed her phone, it was 3:35 in the morning, and she didn't know what the hell she was going to do with Blow's body. Fear began to take over her and she started to panic. She didn't want to go to jail, so she tried to figure out what to do. The thought of self-defense entered her mind, but she was smart enough to know those lines were thin. There was no paper trail of the abuse, and she still might get some time in jail. Kentay popped into her head so she sent him a text and surprisingly, he texted back right away.

Kya: *I need help*

Kentay: *What up?*

Kya: I really need some help. Come to this address as soon as you can. Can't text or talk

Kentay: This ain't no setup or no shit is it?

Kya: NO. I know you can help me though.

Kentay: Bet. I'm not too far away from there anyway

Almost an hour later, Kya heard a vehicle pull up. She wasted no time going to outside because she knew that Kentay was going to be hesitant about coming inside.

"Damn… did that nigga beat you like that?" Tay said as soon as Kya was close.

"Yeah, and I need your help because I don't wanna go to jail," Kya told him and then explained everything that had gone down. She knew that Kentay wouldn't have a problem helping her out because of the incident he had with Blow that one time. He made some phone calls and thirty minutes later, some of his people were pulling up to handle the situation. Kentay never stepped foot in the house, but he handled the situation for Kya.

"You need a ride somewhere? To the hospital?" Kentay asked her after everything was over.

"Just back to my room. My car is there. I'll be okay," she told him and gave him the address. They rode back to campus in silence. Kya was glad everything was over and prayed nothing would come back to haunt her. "Thank you Tay. I owe you," Kya said and got out once Kentay pulled up on campus.

Chapter Thirty-Two

Three Months Later...

"Are we ever going to meet her mother?" the lady asked Jason while he was picking Kendra up from the babysitter.

"Very soon," Jason replied and tried to leave in a hurry but the lady wasn't done with him.

"Kendra is a very good baby, but I can't help but to notice that there's something she is missing. When you look deep into her eyes you can see it," the babysitter spoke.

"Her mom died while giving birth. It has been a little hard on me, but I'm doing the best that I can do for her," Jason softly stated. He knew that he had touched a soft spot Ms. Emma's heart when her hands went straight to her mouth and she gasped.

"I'm so sorry to hear that. I know you only allow me to keep her while you're running errands for an hour or two at a time, but I am willing to do more whenever you need me. Don't hesitate to call me," Ms. Emma honestly told him.

"Thank you so much for that, but we're about to be moving soon. I really appreciate everything that you have done," Jason told her. They talked for another minute or two, and Jason left. He felt a little bad about lying to Ms. Emma, but he had to tell her something to get her off of his back.

For the past five months, he had been caring for Kendra just as he said he would. After buying several home DNA kits, he just couldn't bring himself to swab her mouth. Deep down, he already knew that she wasn't his biological child. Staring into her face confirmed it. While watching the Maury show the other day, Jason began to realize that he had made a mistake by taking Kendra and neglecting her from her biological parents without giving them a chance to be parents. It pissed him off to know that Raven had given herself to another man and had a child with him. By him running off, he felt like they had gotten off too easy, which was why he decided to take Kendra back and make other plans for his life.

A couple of months ago, Jason started sending Raven random pictures and messages from an app to let her know that the baby was fine. She repeatedly asked for a location, but he would never tell her that he was still in Oktibbeha County. He was located down near the county lake at his great grandmother's house that no one lived in. He kept the house up and didn't worry about anyone ever seeing him because it was so secluded and couldn't be seen from the road. Raven wouldn't know where he was until he went back to her apartment to get his life, as well as hers together. The plan had been forming in Jason's head for about a week or two now, and he felt like it was now or never. Jason had changed Kendra's pediatrician to one in Columbus and had been taking her for check-ups as needed. She was a good baby, but he couldn't help but to feel bad for her future. The thing that really scared him was the month before when Kendra got sick and Jason panicked. Her cries were uncontrollable and she was hot with a constant fever for about three days straight. Jason did all he could to keep her calm, but he knew she needed medical attention and finally took her to the doctor. When he was asked about the mother's blood type as well as his, he didn't have any answers. Sweet talking the nurse, he was able to get Kendra the proper care she needed, and she has been fine ever since. After several tests were administered, it was determined that Kendra only had a bad reaction to the formula she was being given. The doctor told Jason that he brought her in right on time. The past months had been a joy to Jason, but he wasn't happy deep inside. He was able to get off through his FMLA policy, but it would be a lie if he said that the entire transition had been easy. Jason wanted a family, and in his mind, a family is what he was going to get by after he took care of a few loose ends.

Bundling Kendra up along with all of the things he had purchased over the last few months, Jason headed to his car. The March winds were blowing through the night air and Jason was glad that he dressed Kendra accordingly. After strapping her in, he got in and took off. Jason kept telling himself over and over that he was doing the right thing, so he willed himself to continue going forward no matter how hard it was. Tears began to water his eyes, but he wouldn't allow them to fall.

"After I do this, I know that everything will turn out okay," Jason said to himself. His thoughts were running so rapid that he didn't know he had steered over into the other lane until he heard a horn sounding repeatedly. Snapping back into reality, Jason focused on the road and then took a glimpse in the rearview mirror and noticed that Kendra was sleeping peacefully.

Twenty short minutes later, Jason was pulling up to his destination. Since it was late at night, he figured he would be able to take care of everything and leave quickly without being spotted. Gathering the bags first, Jason went and sat them beside the door. Checking his surroundings and noticing that the coast was clear, he went back to the car and grabbed Kendra. He left her in her car seat, and went and sat her beside the door.

"This is where you belong. If it's meant to be, you will come back to me," he told Kendra and gave her a kiss on the forehead as she continued to sleep. He hoped that the dose of Benadryl would keep her sleep for a few hours until she was discovered. After knocking on the door, Jason quickly left and never looked back.

Chapter Thirty-Three

"If you make us miss our flight, you gon' have to catch these hands," Ashanti said to Aaliyah while they were parking at the airport.

"It ain't all my fault, but we good girl," Liyah replied. They were flying out of the Golden Triangle Regional Airport headed to New York for the championship game. Ashanti never cared for basketball before, but after meeting Ahmad she was all in. March Madness was in full effect and she was loving it. Mississippi State made it to the sweet sixteen, then on to the elite eight, final four, and then made it to the championship. There was no way Ashanti or Aaliyah was going to the miss the game. Aaliyah and Seth had gotten pretty close and that made everything easier for Ashanti because she had an alibi for everything.

Ahmad got them tickets to the game and offered to pay for their flights, but Ashanti declined and purchased for her and Aaliyah. She told Kentay that she was going on a girl's trip to New York, which was partially true. Her friend was with her, and she knew that they would hang out and shop a little while there. To her pleasure, Kentay didn't ask any questions. He just told Ashanti to enjoy herself and she was thankful she didn't have to answer any questions.

Ten minutes later, they turned into the airport, parked, and pretty much ran because they only had thirty minutes before their flight left. Ashanti prayed the whole time that they would make it and had faith that they would since the airport was so small and not many people flew out of it. Her prayer was answered because they made it to the gate just in time. Out of breath, they both took their seats and prepared for takeoff. Ashanti put her headphones in and planned on finishing the last few chapters of "My Shawty" by Twyla T and then sleeping the remainder of the flight. She was in love with Babyface, Chyna, Leah, and Vice, and purposely started reading slow because she didn't want the story to end. Aaliyah purchased the Wi-Fi and said she was going to catch up on some shows on Netflix.

Liyah didn't read like Ashanti so Shanti told her to start with "We Both Can't Be Bae" by Twyla T and promised her that she would turn into an avid reader. Aaliyah bought the books and said that she would read them after she caught up all of her shows.

Ashanti felt someone nudging her and when she opened her eyes, it was Liyah.

"Come on sleepy head. We're here," Aaliyah said while standing up. Ashanti stretched, stood and followed behind her friend to exit the plane. When they made it outside, the New York wind was still a little chilly in March, and they were glad they had on long sleeve MSU shirts. They had to represent their basketball team. Ashanti couldn't wait until the game to wear her custom made shirt by Tiffany Gibbs. When she saw the Facebook page, 'Just An Xpression' and noticed all of the custom made shirts, she hit Tiffany up immediately and was hooked up in a few days. To make it even better, Tiffany's hair was banging and she recommended Ashanti to her cousin. Krystal MzTrecie Gibbs hooked Ashanti and Aaliyah up, and they knew they were flawless as they stepped into the Big Apple.

Since the championship game was at the Madison Square Garden, the team was staying at Kimpton Hotel Eventi, so Ashanti booked their room there as well. The game was scheduled for 8:00 that night, and it was only noon, so they had plenty of time to chill and relax before getting ready and heading there. Once they made it to the hotel and checked in, the girls went up to their rooms and kicked back for a minute. They mapped out their day and decided to go and eat at Parker and Quinn about 2:00, sightsee for an hour or so, and then head back to the room to get ready for the game.

The time flew by, and at 7:00, Ashanti and Aaliyah entered Madison Square Garden, and they saw Mississippi State attire everywhere. When Ashanti noticed the same chick that kept popping up at every game, she got a little salty. She knew that Ahmad wasn't her man, but she couldn't help but to feel some type of way. Liyah noticed her sudden change in mood because she nudged her and cheered her up by pointing to a poster with Ahmad on it stating that he would be a number one draft pick. Ashanti smiled and told herself that the games were over. She wanted to be with Ahmad and would let him know later that night after the game.

Sitting in their courtside seats, all eyes were on Ashanti and Aaliyah. They tried their best to downplay the attention, but it was inevitable. Every now and then, they would look up at the big screen and notice that the camera stayed in their section. Right before tipoff, the cameraman even caught Ashanti blowing Ahmad a kiss. She felt like a teenager with her first crush sitting courtside ready to capture some moments to post on Snap Chat and keep in her phone.

After a nail biting double overtime game, Ahmad hit a three pointer from Seth's assist at the buzzer for the win and the crowd went wild. Confetti fell from the ceiling and cheering was nonstop. To see the look of joy on Ahmad's face made Ashanti's heart melt. She knew that he was doing what he loved and what he was destined for. Reporters kept stopping him for interviews, but he finally got away from them, made his way over to Ashanti and picked her up into a bear hug. When he put her down, Ashanti found herself kissing Ahmad, and the kiss seemed to last forever. Cameras were flashing from everywhere, and she felt like she was right where she was supposed to be.

***

"I got 10 racks on this fight," Tay said after talking it over with Slick.

"Wanna double that?" one of the opponents challenged.

"You ain't said nothing but a word," Kentay said while smirking and pulling his money from his pocket. They were at a dog fight at a secret location outside of Memphis and the fight of the night was about to go down within the next ten to fifteen minutes. The only light that was shining was the light that was placed in the makeshift dog pin. Slick bought his pit bull out and the other guy made his way towards the ring. The dogs were weighed again and a few minutes later, they were in the ring tearing each other apart, but Slicks's pit was winning.

Out of nowhere, blue lights could be seen in the distance and everyone took off running. It had been a minute since a fight had got busted up, but everyone knew that they were on their own if and when it ever happened. Cops swarmed the place and Kentay saw some people get taken down, but he never stopped running. He ran to a hideout spot about five blocks over and tried to catch his breath before going any further. Not knowing which way Slick went, Tay hoped that he had gotten away too. They were in different vehicles and the only thing Kentay could do was wait for a call and pray that it didn't come from the jailhouse.

Three hours later, Kentay was at Ashanti's condo still waiting to hear from Slick. He stopped by the liquor store and picked up some Tennessee Honey and had drank half of the bottle. The championship game was showing on the TV, but Tay couldn't focus on it. The ringing of his phone startled him. When he saw Slick's name pop up on the screen, Tay answered right away.

"What's up dawg?" Tay said right after he swiped to connect the call.

"Damn bruh… it took me for fuckin' ever to get away, but I'm good," Slick replied.

"Nigga I see… long as you good though," Tay replied.

"They got quite a few, but you know how it go. We gotta wait til tomorrow to find out exactly who," Slick retorted. "But hey, I'll be back that way tomorrow my nigga," he continued.

"Bet," Kentay responded and then hung up.

After hearing that Slick was good, Kentay could relax his mind. He flipped on the TV and turned to ESPN. It was his initial plan to catch the basketball game, but shit just kept popping up. Slick pretty much forced him to go to the dog fight after he was going to just do something he hadn't done in a long time, chill out and relax. The game was at halftime and was tied up when Tay tuned in so he went to the kitchen and made two turkey and cheese sandwiches, grabbed a bag of Doritos out of the cabinet, and went and sat back down. He still had some Hennessy left so he didn't need anything else. By the time the game came back on, he was done with his food and ready to watch the game.

The first person the camera landed on was Ahmad Jones, and Kentay hated that he hadn't personally met him yet or saw him ball out up close and personal. Before the third quarter started, an overview of the crowd displayed on the screen and Ashanti and Aaliyah were among the first to be seen, but Kentay missed it while he was throwing back a shot.

"This duo for the Mississippi State Bulldogs has been unstoppable pretty much all season," the announcer said in reference to Ahmad and Seth. Kentay saw exactly what he meant as he continued to watch the game.

The game went into double overtime, and Tay never moved from his seat, he was so engaged in. When Ahmad shot the three for the win at the buzzer, Tay jumped up like he had made the shot. He had a feeling of proudness and couldn't wait to meet the young guy. The doorbell rang and Kentay wondered who in the hell could be at the door since Ashanti was gone. Picking up the bottle of Hennessy, he was about to down the rest of it until he saw a familiar face on the TV screen.

"What the entire fuck?" he yelled after the camera zoomed in on Ashanti. When he witnessed Ashanti kissing Ahmad after he picked her up and placed her back down on the floor, Kentay stood in her living room and slammed the entire bottle he was holding into the glass table. The table shattered along with the bottle, and the remaining liquor spilled out. Tay went into a frenzied fit after watching the woman he loved kiss and be so close and familiar with another man. He found himself breaking shit before he caught himself.

"I warned her ass. I told her I would kill any muthafuckin' man she got involved with. Fuuuccckkk! It's a muthafuckin' shame that Ima have to kill my own got damn brother! You're mine, Shanti. I'm not about to let you go, I don't give a damn what you say. This shit ain't gon' fly," Tay raged to himself as he paced back and forth before grabbing his keys to head out of the door with vengeance on his mind. After opening the door, he walked out and tripped, almost falling completely over. After finding his balance and righting himself upright, Kentay looked down to see what kind of object caused him to almost bust his ass. His mouth dropped opened wide when he realized that he was stopped by some bags and a baby in a car seat. "Da hell? What kind of fuckery is this? Where in the hell did she come from?" Tay yelled as he stood mesmerized and puzzled by the sudden appearance of the baby…Raven's baby…his baby!

To Be Continued…

Note From The Author:

I really hope you all enjoyed part one of my new series. I really enjoyed bringing these characters to life. It seemed like so much was riding on this book, but I prayed, wrote, and hope I delivered a story that you all loved.

As always, I would love to have your honest feedback to help me excel in my passion. When you are done, please leave me a review on Amazon, Good Reads, and/or any of my social media and I will reply. My Facebook, Instagram, and Twitter handles are all @authortwylat

You may also email me at authortwylat@gmail.com

Search Twyla T's Reading Group on Facebook if you love my work and become a supporter!

Other great reads by Author Twyla T.

We Both Can't Be Bae 1-3

I'll Never Love A Dope Boy Again 1-2

My Shawty: An Original Love Story 1-3 (Pinned under TWYLA, but it's mine)

Made in the USA
Coppell, TX
08 December 2020